Writing from Australia

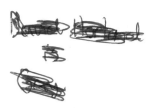

Figures in a Landscape

Figures in a Landscape

Writing from Australia

Wendy Morgan

CAMBRIDGE
UNIVERSITY PRESS

Published by the Press Syndicate of the University of Cambridge

The Pitt Building, Trumpington Street, Cambridge CB2 IRP

40 West 20th Street, New York, NY 10011-4211, USA

10 Stamford Road, Oakleigh, Melbourne 3166, Australia

First published 1994

Printed in Great Britain at the University Press, Cambridge

A catalogue record for this book is available from the British Library

Library of Congress cataloguing in publication data

ISBN 0 521 42150 0 paperback

VN

Contents

Acknowledgements

A number of people have helped me in the lengthy business of choosing the stories and pictures which make up this book. I owe thanks to the students of my English classes at Wilderness School, Adelaide, South Australia, who read so many stories and taught me much as they shared their responses with me and with one another; to my colleagues on the South Australian Education Department Exploring and Connecting Texts task group, who read numerous stories and gave me the benefit of their thoughtful reading and sharp understanding of what would work best in English classrooms: Peter Adams, Brian Bates, Jacqui Howard, Chris Thomson; especially to Loris Waller of Wilderness School, for her time and care, expertise and imagination in selecting such unexpectedly right images for this volume; and above all to Mike Hayhoe, the editor of the series, for his attention to detail, his energy and enthusiasm, his acute judgement – and his many friendly letters.

Thanks are due to the following for permission to reproduce illustrations: p. xiv, p. 14, p. 66, p. 126 and p. 142 National Gallery of Australia, Canberra; p. 4 John Williams; p. 8 Kay Lawrence, photograph supplied by Wilderness School, Australia; p. 26 Peter Lyssiotis; p. 36 Campfire Group (in collaboration with Michael Eather) Queensland; p. 48 Queensland University of Technology Art Collection, Brisbane; p. 54 National Gallery of Victoria, Melbourne; p. 75 Art Gallery of Western Australia; p. 80 Artlink, Scan +; p. 86 Niagara Galleries, Private Collection, Melbourne; p. 102 Ron Hawke; p. 113 Barbara Hanrahan and Wakefield Press, (Aust) Pty; p. 122 Richard Tipping; p. 149 Geoff Parr.

Thanks are due to the following for permission to reproduce stories: p. 1 'Three Lizards Dreaming' by Obed Raggett in *Stories of Obed Raggett*, 1980, pp. 69–72, Alternative Publishing Cooperative, Chippendale, Sydney, NSW; p. 3 'Neighbours' by Tim Winton used by permission of Australian Literary Management, 2a Armstrong Street, Middle Park, Victoria 3206; p. 9 'The Children' from *Stories of the Waterfront* by John Morrison in Penguin Best Australian Short Stories, edited by Mary Lord, 1991, pp. 227–31, Penguin Books Australia Ltd; p. 15 'Legs by Elizabeth Dean © Elizabeth Dean; p. 25 'Teach me to Dance' by Kerryn Goldsworthy, 1989, reprinted by permission of McPhee Gribble; p. 35 'One of My Best Friends' by Peter Goldsworthy © Peter Goldsworthy; p. 42 'Paradise' by Murray Bail in *Contemporary Portraits*, 1975, pp. 115–22, University of Queensland Press; p. 49 'The Piece of Pork' by Mr Tan in *People and Stories* from Indo-China, edited by Morag Loh, 1982, pp. 41–44, Indo-China Refugee Association of Victoria; p. 53 'Going Home' from *Going Home* by Archie Weller, 1986, pp. 1–11, Allen Unwin; p. 65 'After the Cut Out' by D'Arcy Niland, permission granted by Kemalde Pty Ltd, care of Curtis Brown (Aust) Pty Ltd, Sydney; p. 73 'Maralinga' by Lallie Lennon © Lallie Lennon; p. 81 'Just Like That' by Michael Richards © Michael Richards; p. 87 'Bill Sprockett's Land' from *Stories* by Elizabeth Jolley © 1976, 1979, 1984 by Elizabeth Jolley, used by permission of Viking Penguin, a division of Penguin Books USA inc. in UK and Canada, permission granted for Australia by Freemantle Arts Centre Press, Western Australia; p. 92 'Telling Tales' from *Miracle of the Waters* by Zeny Giles, permission granted by Penguin Books

Australia Ltd; p. 97 'The Larder' by Morris Lurie © Morris Lurie; p. 101 'Warrigal' by Dal Stivens © Dal Stivens; p. 111 'Day trip to Surfers b/w Get Lost Adorno' by Craig McGregor in *Real Lies*, 1987, pp. 1–13, University of Queensland Press; p. 123 'Wogs' by Ania Walwicz in *Mattoid* 13, 1982, pp. 16–17; p. 125 'The Three Legged Bitch' by Alan Marshall, used by permission of Curtis Brown (Aust) Pty Ltd, Sydney; p. 143 'We Like White Man Alright' by Bill Neidjie in *Story About Feeling*, Bill Neidjie, 1989, pp. 163–71 used by permission of Magabala Books, Aboriginal Corporation, Broome, Western Australia.

Every attempt has been made to locate copyright holders for all material in this book. The publishers would be glad to hear from anyone whose copyright has been unwittingly infringed.

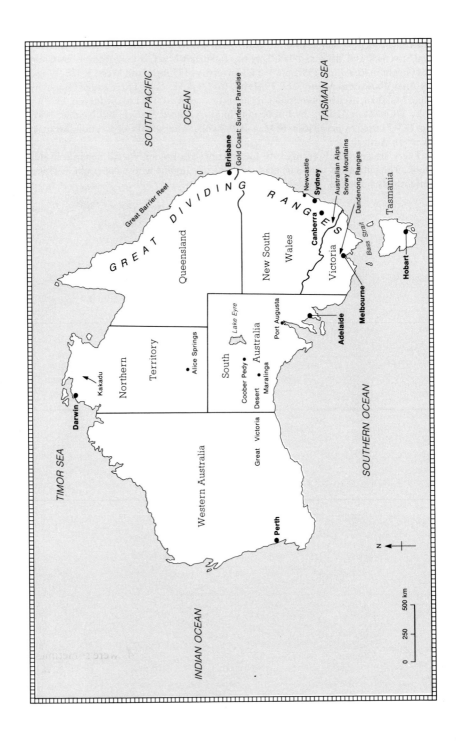

Introduction

Towards the end of the eighteenth century, Europeans – explorers, invaders, colonisers – sailed to that great island continent in the south they called Australia. But that was not the beginning of the story, even though the newcomers thought they were starting afresh, in a land that was like a blank sheet of paper. They called it *terra nullius* – the uninhabited land, the land that belongs to no one. (This idea or concept of *terra nullius*, a land no one had a claim on, has recently been revoked by a legal decision which has far-reaching consequences for the claims of Aboriginal peoples to their right to their traditional sacred lands.) The phrase *terra nullius* did not just describe the land as those first Europeans saw it. It enabled them to think of that 'empty' land as theirs for the taking; to assume it had no peoples, no history or stories; and to push the Aboriginal peoples to the margins of the whites' country, whites' history and stories, even though these peoples had inhabited the land successfully for tens of thousands of years.

The land of those original inhabitants was not of course divided by boundaries into eight states or territories. It was marked out in other ways. As they travelled back and forth over their landscapes, the Aboriginal peoples retold stories about the various places they came to. In this way they 'read' their country like the text of a story or playscript or an ongoing conversation. They did not claim to own the land and did not talk about possessing it and guarding their boundaries; the land and they lived together. And their words gave their meanings to the land: words used to describe, create, imagine, explain – and in more than 250 Aboriginal languages.

Australia today is saturated with the English language, and only about twenty-five of the original languages are still actively used and taught to Aboriginal children. However, a number of words from various Aboriginal languages have become common in English, mostly those that name animals and plants, such as *koala* or *kangaroo*, *mallee* or *waratah*, or implements, such as *boomerang*. And a large number of Aboriginal place names across Australia, from *Andamooka* to *Geelong* to *Woolloomooloo*, record the traces of the people who first knew the land. (These words were sometimes misheard or underwent odd changes when they were written down in the English alphabet.)

Words were used very differently by those early European settlers, who came to this land as unwilling convicts sent out to a prison-country, or as gaolers and soldiers, or as free settlers keen to make a new life and a profit from the place. These people brought their English language to Australia and tried to make it fit a landscape that was very different from what they'd known. For example, a 'robin', or a 'creek' or an 'oak' is not at all the same here as in England. The native flame robins, scarlet robins, or red-capped robins, are more vivid in colour and song than their English namesake. A 'creek' in England is a narrow recess in the shore of the sea, a small inlet or bay, whereas in Australia it is a stream, the branch of a river, and may be more than a thousand kilometres inland. And a 'she-oak' is a *Casuarina*, with long needles for leaves, while a 'silky oak' is a *Grevillea robusta*, an upright tree with fern-like foliage and bright orange flowers in spring.

The 'fit' between English words and Australian things could never be perfect – especially in a place where people felt dis-placed. In time, English-speaking Australians have made the place their own and their language seems comfortable, even natural. But in their language it is a different place from what the Aboriginal inhabitants had known.

You could say there's no such place as Australia; that there are only various places that people have talked and written about and depicted in images. People – figures – make the landscape they live in by representing it to themselves and others in certain ways, in words and pictures and stories.

Many tourists – and many Australians, looking at television advertise-ments or glossy coffee-table books – may still think of Australia as a place of huge hot sandy deserts inhabited by kangaroos and emus, or hot dry forests with koalas and the cackle of kookaburras or the crackle of a bushfire, or vast stretches of hot white sand lapped by brilliantly blue waves and shaded by palm trees. And for contrast there are the white sails of the Sydney Opera House, and the skyscrapers of modern cities or the high-rise apartments at resorts on the Gold Coast. . . . Certainly these are aspects of Australia today, and no one Australian can know it all, from the tropical north with its monsoon storms to Tasmania in the south with its winter snows. But many Australians have their own Australia which they know well and can tell stories about, whether it includes tree ferns in tropical Queensland rainfor-ests or Hills hoists (rotary clothes-lines) in back yards across the suburbs that sprawl for miles around the cities; whether it involves trams in Melbourne or chairlifts on the mountainous snowfields of Victoria; gelati or baklava in inner-city delis (corner stores) or lamingtons in small town cake shops; the roar of grand prix races or of crowds at rock concerts . . .

In the stories here you will not experience the 'real' Australia directly; however, you will find various ways of being Australian represented here: particular ways of knowing, believing, thinking and feeling. These stories will not give you the 'truth' about Australia: the writers are more interested in asking questions about the things Australians have taken for granted as the truth about who they are, where and how they live.

Who are 'Australians' now? Among their number are people who have immigrated to this country in recent years. Especially after the Second World War, many people came from Europe to live in Australia ('new Australians', they were then called, mainly from Italy, Greece, and also from more northern European nations). And in later years numbers of people have immigrated from various parts of the Asia-Pacific region. They have added their stories to all the writing that officially or unofficially tells Australians who they are and what their place is in this place together, and in the world.

As you will see when you read the stories in this book, the faces of the country and the nation continue to change – and so do its languages. In these pages you will meet the particular ways of talking that are shared by an older generation in Australia, by young people, or people in certain jobs or with certain views. You will meet some varieties of Aboriginal English – forms of English which these peoples have taken up and developed in different ways, to suit their own culture and purposes as Aborigines in an English-dominated society. And you will meet other varieties of Australian English, spoken by members of more than ninety culturally distinct immigrant groups that speak more than thirty languages other than English.

As the editor responsible for selecting these stories, which I've chosen from more than a hundred books and dozens of magazines, I had a problem: what was I going to exclude, when my aim was to include as much as possible of the varieties of Australian ways of telling and seeing? I can only hope that my chosen stories will suggest something of that variety. For example, I have not included any stories from the convict days (though Bill Neidjie makes a telling point about the chains used on convicts and blacks alike); however, you might be able to see the experiences and attitudes of those times as a theme running through some of the stories in this book – especially those stories that celebrate rebellion against the authorities and take as their heroes those who have failed rather than succeeded. (Perhaps this refusal to respect the power of a 'ruling class' explains why so many Australians dot their speech with vulgar or obscene or blasphemous words, without meaning to shock or offend the person they're speaking to.) These stories and others explore and question what has been taken as characteristic of 'the' Australian character. And you too can read to question what many Australians have taken for granted, because of your own background and experiences, which may be very different from what you are given in the stories.

So what topics of Australian-ness will you find, and find questioned, in my selection? (You can identify your own examples in the stories as you read, and you will make links between stories in addition to those suggested in the introductions.) But in all that you read, remember that these are versions, fictions; they will not give you Australian experiences directly, nor accurate information which you can take simply as the truth.

Here are traditional or more recent stories by Aborigines, some originally told aloud, some written. They tell of Aborigines as victimised or triumphing over repression or prejudice, of Aborigines living wisely in their own land. The ongoing story of relations between black and white in Australia is not resolved yet: but you will find depicted in these stories something of the conditions that will affect what happens in the future.

You will read here stories of white settlers in a land they regarded as harsh and hostile – a land to be fought against or endured. In many older stories the responses of these pioneers to their hardships were presented as characteristically Australian: they were shown as brave, tough in body and spirit, and not given to complaining. This myth in praise of the pioneer is questioned in a number of stories here. You will read of settlers longing for a fertile land where they can build happy homes and lead independent lives – dreams tested by experience. Such stories represent the cost of bravery or failure of nerve, the limitations of 'mateship' (where men put loyalty to their male friends above everything else), and the consequences of the settlers' hostility to the land and its animals.

These days, however, the great majority of Australians live in cities and large towns. Many of them work in offices. And many are not able to find any work, fulfilling or not. What do they aspire to in their dreams of the good life? Several stories take up this issue. People in the suburbs, no less than in the outback, can feel territorial – or isolated and out of place. What sorts of comforts do they find, and are these comforts satisfying only if they do not look beneath the surface of their lives? Families are represented here too in some of their varieties: families whose members are loyal and supportive (though relations will always be complicated), and other families whose members disappoint, warp or betray one another. How have such families, in various times and places and circumstances, affected the ways girls and boys grow up and think of themselves as women and men? And when people grow old, will they be able to maintain their independence within a safety net of support and respect, or will they confront loneliness and loss of dignity?

Australia's cities have multiculturally diverse populations. When people of various ethnic groups live in close contact, their differences may cause suspicion and grievance and rejection or may be an opportunity to learn and grow and become different from who they once were. Here too the older members of each generation may find their ways of life changing: the old habits and old stories of their homeland become new in a new situation.

New stories to tell may need new ways of telling. Among the stories collected here you will find not only a range of subjects but also a range of forms. Some are the kinds of stories you may know well: believable stories with a clear beginning, a series of events in the middle and an ending that 'wraps it up' neatly. Other stories do not obey this pattern. They take the form of letters, stories within stories, recorded conversations; and in one case at the end of the story each of the characters tells how he or she 'read', or interpreted, it. When *you* read and talk about these stories you will be doing the same sort of thing: re-creating and interpreting them, re-presenting for yourself these ways of representing some of the varieties of Australian figures in a landscape.

Wendy Morgan
Brisbane, Queensland

Wandjuk Marika, Dhangu, Rirratjungu clan,
1927–87. *The Clans, Djang'kawu Children, 1982*,
ochres on eucalyptus bark, 126.0 × 34.0 cm.

Three Lizard Dreamings

OBED RAGGETT   1980

This is a traditional Aboriginal tale, a *Tjukurpa*, a story of the
'Dreaming'. Many of these kinds of tale explain how certain animals
came to have their present forms. This one, about three big lizards
(*goannas*), is told in various ways across central Australia. Obed
Raggett, of the Aranda people, has translated his version into English.

Another traditional story is told in 'The Piece of Pork', page 49.

Once upon a time there were three great lizards. They looked the same; they
were the same size; they talked the same and they called themselves 'men'.
They were called (Prenti) Goanna, (Black) Goanna, and Goanna.

One day they were talking about painting, and about painting themselves.
Prenti Goanna said: 'We must paint ourselves properly with paint.'

'Oh yes,' Goanna said.

'That's right,' Prenti Goanna said, 'and first, you two must paint me!'

With this they all made ready to paint Prenti Goanna. First they got
charcoal, then white ochre and red ochre. Then they set to work and painted
Prenti Goanna.

Now, they painted that Prenti Goanna very carefully, so that he looked
very good. However, Prenti Goanna didn't like the way they had painted him.
'No! This is no good. You two have been fooling with me. I'm not at all happy
with this. Look! I'm black all over! I look terrible,' he sulked.

So then they decided to paint Black Goanna. They collected charcoal, some
prickles and just a little white ochre. Then they painted Black Goanna's nose;
they painted it black. After that, they painted him black all over. Then they
put prickles on him and rolled him over and over in the prickles and in the
charcoal. Soon they had made him into a big mess with prickles and charcoal
all over. He has been like that ever since.

Prenti Goanna, still angry at the way he had been painted, said 'You'll be a
small black lizard for ever, Black Goanna – not like me!' Then using his
magic, Prenti made Black Goanna into a small, black lizard.

Last of all they made ready to paint Goanna. They collected sand, some red
ochre and some white ochre. They didn't get any charcoal. First they put

paint on Goanna, all over him. Then they rolled Goanna in the sand so that he had sand all over him. He looked like a big, sandy mess!

Having finished their painting, and having put away all the paint, Prenti said to Black Goanna (now, Black Lizard): 'You're too small! You go away and live beside the creeks in hollow trees. That's your place now!'

Then, to Goanna, he said: 'You've been painted like sand, you'll have to go away too! You go and make your place in the sand (hills). I'm making you small from now on also. You're not like me anymore; go away you sand goanna!'

So Prenti Goanna, Black Lizard and Sand Goanna weren't friends anymore (and didn't call themselves men), and only Prenti Goanna wandered everywhere.

Neighbours

TIM WINTON   1985

'When they first moved in, the young couple were wary of the neighbourhood. The street was full of European migrants.'

In this story, set in the inner suburbs of an Australian city, families from different ethnic and cultural groups gradually come to interact in new ways, to become 'neighbourly'.
   Tim Winton is a writer from Western Australia who has been writing novels and short stories full time since he was twenty-two.

'Warrigal', page 101, tells the story of a very different suburban community.

When they first moved in, the young couple were wary of the neighbourhood. The street was full of European migrants. It made the newly-weds feel like sojourners in a foreign land. Next door on the left lived a Macedonian family. On the right, a widower from Poland.

The newly-weds' house was small, but its high ceilings and paned windows gave it the feel of an elegant cottage. From his study window, the young man could see out over the rooftops and used-car yards the Moreton Bay figs in the park where they walked their dog. The neighbours seemed cautious about the dog, a docile, moulting collie.

The young man and woman had lived all their lives in the expansive outer suburbs where good neighbours were seldom seen and never heard. The sounds of spitting and washing and daybreak watering came as a shock. The Macedonian family shouted, ranted, screamed. It took six months for the newcomers to comprehend the fact that their neighbours were not murdering each other, merely talking. The old Polish man spent most of his day hammering nails into wood only to pull them out again. His yard was stacked with salvaged lumber. He added to it, but he did not build with it.

Relations were uncomfortable for many months. The Macedonians raised eyebrows at the late hour at which the newcomers rose in the mornings. The young man sensed their disapproval at his staying home to write his thesis while his wife worked. He watched in disgust as the little boy next door urinated in the street. He once saw him spraying the cat from the back step.

Paddington, Sydney 1962 by John Williams.

The child's head was shaved regularly, he assumed, in order to make his hair grow thick. The little boy stood at the fence with only his cobalt eyes showing; it made the young man nervous.

In the autumn, the young couple cleared rubbish from their back yard and turned and manured the soil under the open and measured gaze of the neighbours. They planted leeks, onions, cabbage, brussels sprouts and broad beans and this caused the neighbours to come to the fence and offer advice about spacing, hilling, mulching. The young man resented the interference, but he took careful note of what was said. His wife was bold enough to run a hand over the child's stubble and the big woman with black eyes and butcher's arms gave her a bagful of garlic cloves to plant.

Not long after, the young man and woman built a henhouse. The neighbours watched it fall down. The Polish widower slid through the fence uninvited and rebuilt it for them. They could not understand a word he said.

As autumn merged into winter and the vermilion sunsets were followed by sudden, dark dusks touched with the smell of woodsmoke and the sound of roosters crowing day's end, the young couple found themselves smiling back at the neighbours. They offered heads of cabbage and took gifts of grappa and firewood. The young man worked steadily at his thesis on the development of the twentieth-century novel. He cooked dinners for his wife and listened to her stories of eccentric patients and hospital incompetence. In the street they no longer walked with their eyes lowered. They felt superior and proud when their parents came to visit and to cast shocked glances across the fence.

In the winter they kept ducks, big, silent muscovies that stood about in the rain growing fat. In the spring the Macedonian family showed them how to slaughter and to pluck and to dress. They all sat around on blocks and upturned buckets and told barely-understood stories – the men butchering, the women plucking, as was demanded. In the haze of down and steam and fractured dialogue, the young man and woman felt intoxicated. The cat toyed with severed heads. The child pulled the cat's tail. The newcomers found themselves shouting.

But they had not planned on a pregnancy. It stunned them to be made parents so early. Their friends did not have children until several years after being married – if at all. The young woman arranged for maternity leave. The young man ploughed on with his thesis on the twentieth-century novel.

The Polish widower began to build. In the late spring dawns, he sank posts and poured cement and began to use his wood. The young couple turned in their bed, cursed him behind his back. The young husband, at times, suspected that the widower was deliberately antagonising them. The young wife threw up in the mornings. Hay fever began to wear him down.

Before long the young couple realised that the whole neighbourhood knew of the pregnancy. People smiled tirelessly at them. The man in the deli gave her small presents of chocolates and him packets of cigarettes that he stored at home, not being a smoker. In the summer, Italian women began to offer names. Greek women stopped the young woman in the street, pulled her skirt up and felt her belly, telling her it was bound to be a boy. By late summer the woman next door had knitted the baby a suit, complete with booties and beanie. The young woman felt flattered, claustrophobic, grateful, peeved.

By late summer, the Polish widower next door had almost finished his two-car garage. The young man could not believe that a man without a car would do such a thing, and one evening as he was considering making a complaint about the noise, the Polish man came over with barrowfuls of wood-scraps for their fire.

Labour came abruptly. The young man abandoned the twentieth-century novel for the telephone. His wife began to black the stove. The midwife came and helped her finish the job while he ran about making statements that sounded like queries. His wife hoisted her belly about the house, supervising his movements. Going outside for more wood, he saw, in the last light of the day, the faces at each fence. He counted twelve faces. The Macedonian family waved and called out what sounded like their best wishes.

As the night deepened, the young woman dozed between contractions, sometimes walking, sometimes shouting. She had a hot bath and began to eat ice and demand liverwurst. Her belly rose, uterus flexing downward. Her sweat sparkled, the gossamer highlit by movement and firelight. The night grew older. The midwife crooned. The young man rubbed his wife's back, fed her ice and rubbed her lips with oil.

And then came the pushing. He caressed and stared and tried not to shout. The floor trembled as the young woman bore down in a squat. He felt the power of her, the sophistication of her. She strained. Her face mottled. She kept at it, push after push, assaulting some unseen barrier, until suddenly it was smashed and she was through. It took his wind away to see the look on the baby's face as it was suddenly passed up to the breast. It had one eye on him. It found the nipple. It trailed cord and vernix smears and its mother's own sweat. She gasped and covered the tiny buttocks with a hand. A boy, she said. For a second, the child lost the nipple and began to cry. The young man heard shouting outside. He went to the back door. On the Macedonian side of the fence, a small queue of bleary faces looked up, cheering, and the young man began to weep. The twentieth-century novel had not prepared him for this.

Crossroad, Crossed Paths, Crossing Out

During a disastrous bushfire in 1983 flames encircled Kay Lawrence's house in the Adelaide Hills. Afterwards, in the desolate, burnt-out landscape, she found criss-crossing animal tracks revealed for the first time. Lawrence used the images of these paths and other crossed roads to explore the idea of choice and decision-making in her own life.

Crossroad, Crossed Paths, Crossing Out by Kay Lawrence, 1983, ink, coloured pencil, photocopy and linen thread on cartridge paper, original image size 6½ inches wide × 5½ inches high.

The Children

JOHN MORRISON   1950

'Here and there people searching the ashes of their homes stood upright and watched with hard and bitter faces.'

John Morrison, who came to Australia from England as a young man, has written many stories about the work and home life of ordinary people. Here a man fighting a bushfire that threatens to engulf a little settlement has a terrible decision to make and live with.

Another man feels isolated from a country town community in 'After the Cut Out', page 65.

He was almost ready to go when I found him. He was, to be exact, engaged in putting the final lashings onto his big truck. Blackened and blistered, and loaded up with all his worldly possessions, it was backed right up to a dry old verandah littered with dead leaves and odds and ends of rubbish. He turned to me as I got near, his bloodshot eyes squinting at me with frank hostility.

'Another newshawk.'

'The *Weekly*, Mr Allen.'

His expression softened a little. 'I've got nothing against the *Weekly*.'

'We thought there might be something more to it,' I said gently. 'We know the dailies never tell a straight story.'

'They did this time,' he replied. 'I'm not making excuses.'

With the dexterity of a man who did it every day, he tied a sheepshank, ran the end of the rope through a ring under the decking, up through the eye of the knot, and back to the ring.

'I've got something to answer for all right,' he said with tight lips. 'But nobody need worry, I'll pay! I'll pay for it all the rest of my life. I'm that way now I can't bear the sight of my own kids.'

I kept silent for a moment. 'We understand that, Mr Allen. We just thought there might be something that hasn't come out yet.'

'No, I wouldn't say there's anything that hasn't come out. It's just that – well, people don't think enough, they don't think, that's all.'

He was facing me now, and looking very much, in his immobility, a part of the great background of desolation. The marks of fire were all over him.

Charred boots, burned patches on his clothes, singed eyebrows, blistered face
and hands, little crusts all over his hat where sparks had fallen. Over his
shoulder the sun was just rising between Hunter and Mabooda Hills, a
monstrous ball of copper glowing and fading behind the waves of smoke still
drifting up from the valley. Fifty yards away the dusty track marked the
western limit of destruction. The ground on this side of it was the first brown
earth I had seen since leaving Burt's Creek; Allen's house the first survivor
after a tragic procession of stark chimney stacks and overturned water tanks.

'It must have been hell!' I said.

'That?' He made a gesture of indifference. 'That's nothing. It'll come good
again. It's the children.'

'I know.'

The door of the house opened. I saw a woman with children at her skirts.
She jumped as she caught sight of me, and in an instant the door banged,
leaving me with an impression of whirling skirts and large frightened eyes.

'The wife's worse than me,' said Allen, 'she can't face anybody.'

He was looking away from me now, frowning and withdrawn, in the way
of a man living something all over again, something he can't leave alone. I
could think of nothing to say which wouldn't sound offensively platitudi-
nous. It was the most unhappy assignment I had ever been given. I couldn't
get out of my mind the hatred in the faces of some men down on the main
road when I'd asked to be directed to the Allen home.

I took out my cigarettes, and was pleased when he accepted one. A man
won't do that if he has decided not to talk to you.

'How did it come to be you?' I asked. 'Did Vince order you to go, or did you
volunteer?' Vince was the foreman ranger in that part of the Dandenongs.

'I didn't ask him, if that's what you mean. I don't work for the
Commission. The truck's my living, I'm a carrier. But everybody's in on a fire,
and Vince is in charge.'

'Vince picked you . . .'

'He picked me because I had the truck with me. I'd been down to the Gully
to bring up more men, and it was parked on the break.'

'Then it isn't true . . .'

'That I looked for the job because of my own kids? No! That's a damned
lie. I didn't even have cause to be worried about my own kids just then. I'm
not trying to get out of it, but there's plenty to blame besides me: the Forestry
Commission, the Education Department, and everybody in Burt's Creek and

Yileena if it comes to that. Those children should never have been there to begin with. They should have been sent down to the Gully on Friday or kept in their homes. The fire was on this side of the reserve right up to noon.'

He wheeled, pointing towards the distant top of Wanga Hill. Through the drifting haze of smoke we could make out the little heap of ruins closely ringed by black and naked spars that had been trees. Here and there along the very crest, where the road ran, the sun glinted now and then on the windscreens of standing cars, morbid sightseers from the city.

'Just look at it!' he said vehemently. 'Timber right up to the fence-lines! A school in a half-acre paddock – in country like this!'

His arm fell. 'But what's the use of talking? I was told to go and get the kids out, and I didn't do it. I got my own. Nothing else matters now.'

'You thought there was time to pick up your own children first, and then go on to the school, Mr Allen?'

'That's about the size of it,' he assented gloomily.

I'd felt all along that he did want to talk to somebody about it. It came now with a rush.

'Nut it out for yourself,' he appealed. 'What your paper says isn't going to make anybody think any different now. But I'll tell you this: there isn't another bloke in the world would have done anything else. I should be shot – I wish to God they would shoot me! – but I'm still no worse than anybody else. I was the one it happened to, that's all. Them people who lost kids have got a perfect right to hate my guts, but supposing it had been one of them? Supposing it had been you . . . what would you have done?'

I just looked at him.

'You know, don't you? In your own heart you know?'

'Yes, I know.'

'The way it worked out you'd think somebody had laid a trap for me. Vince had got word that the fire had jumped the main road and was working up the far side of Wanga. And he told me to take the truck and make sure the kids had been got away from the school. All right – now follow me. I get started. I come along the low road there. I get the idea right away that I'll pick up my own wife and kids afterwards. But when I reach that bit of open country near Hagen's bridge when you can see Wanga, I look up. And, so help me God! there's smoke. Now that can mean only one thing: that the Burt's Creek leg of the fire has jumped the Government break and is heading this way. Think that one over. I can see the very roof of my house, and there's smoke showing at the back of it. I know there's scrub right up to the fences, and I've got a wife and kids there. The other way there's twenty kids, but there's no smoke showing yet. And the wind's in the north-east. And I'm in a good truck. And there's a fair track right through from my place to the school. What would you expect me to do?'

He would see the answer in my face.

'There was the choice,' he said with dignified finality. 'One way, my own two kids. The other way, twenty kids that weren't mine. That's how everybody sees it, just as simple as that.'

'When did you first realise you were too late for the school?'

'As soon as I pulled up here. My wife had seen me coming and was outside with the kids and a couple of bundles. She ran up to the truck as I stopped, shouting and pointing behind me.' He closed his eyes and shivered. 'When I put my head out at the side and looked back I couldn't see the school. A bloke just above the creek had a lot of fern and blackberry cut, all ready for burning off. The fire had got into that and was right across the bottom of Wanga in the time it took me to get to my place from the road. The school never had a hope. Some of the kids got up as far as the road, but it's not very wide and there was heavy fern right out to the metal.'

I waited, while he closed his eyes and shook his head slowly from side to side.

'I'd have gone through, though, just the same, if it hadn't been for the wife. She'll tell you. We had a fight down there where the tracks branch. I had the truck flat out and headed for Wanga. I knew what it meant, but I'd have done it. I got it into my head there was nothing else to do but cremate the lot, truck and everything in it. But the wife grabbed the wheel. It's a wonder we didn't leave the road.'

'You turned back . . .'

'Yes, damn my soul! I turned back. There was fire everywhere. Look at the truck. The road was alight both sides all the way back to Hagen's. Just the same, it would have been better if we'd gone on.'

That, I felt, was the simple truth, his own two innocents notwithstanding. I had an impulse to ask him what happened when he reached Burt's Creek, but restrained myself. His shame was painful to witness.

A minute or two later I said goodbye. He was reluctant to take my hand.

'I kept trying to tell myself somebody else might have got the kids out,' he whispered. 'But nobody did. Word had got around somehow that the school had been evacuated. Only the teacher – they found her with a bunch of them half a mile down the road. And to top it all off my own place got missed! That bit of cultivation down there – you wouldn't read about it, would you?'

No, you wouldn't read about it.

In the afternoon, at the Gully, standing near the ruins of the hotel, I saw him passing. A big fire-scarred truck rolling slowly down the debris-littered road. Behind the dirty windscreen one could just discern the hunted faces of a man and woman. Two children peeped out of a torn side-curtain. Here and there people searching the ashes of their homes stood upright and watched with hard and bitter faces.

SŎL'ĬTARĬ, LIVING ALONE, NOT GREGARIOUS, WITHOUT COMPANIONS,UNFREQUENTED, SECLUDED, SINGLE, LONELY. SŎL'STICĔ, EITHER TIME (SUMMER,WINTER) AT WHICH SUN IS FARTHEST FROM EQUATOR AND APPEARS TO PAUSE BEFORE RETURNING. SŎL'US, (FEM.SOLA). ALONE, UNACCOMPANIED. SŎLVE, UNTIE, LOOSEN, UNRAVEL, DISSOLVE; FIND ANSWER TO (PROBLEM) OR WAY OUT. HENCE SŎL'VABLE AGAIN.

Bea Maddock, Australia, born 1934, *Solitary*, 1979, encaustic and collage on canvas, 183.5 × 153.0 cm.
Collection: National Gallery of Australia, Canberra.

Legs

ELIZABETH DEAN   1983

'Probably trying to be a smart arse. When the computer rejects and he doesn't get his cheque, it will be a different story.'

'As this department has spent considerable time at the taxpayers' expense on your case in trying to help you to receive your entitlement under the Act, there is nothing further we are able to do for you, unless you agree to the criteria under which we operate.
Yours faithfully, etc.'

In Australia currently, many people are unable to find work. In this story an unemployed man challenges the officials of the government department that organises unemployment relief payments. What will it take to arrive at a solution everyone finds satisfactory?

Elizabeth Dean has been a social worker and full-time writer since 1983.

In 'Paradise', page 42, another man uses written words in ways that bureaucrats did not intend.

'Read this letter,' Barra said to Fiona. 'This man's a nut.' Fiona took the sheet of lined paper and scanned the neat, almost copperplate handwriting. Frowning, her lips moving soundlessly, she read:

Dear Sir,

So that you may change your records, I would like you to know I have changed my name by deed poll to Legs. I no longer answer to any other name. I would be grateful if you would address any future correspondence to this name. Of course this will include my unemployment cheque. I have notified my bank and other business connections of my change of name.

I hope you will not be inconvenienced too much as I would dislike to put you to any extra trouble. I am very grateful to your department for providing me with a regular pittance. I enclose a copy of the deed poll.
Yours sincerely,
Legs.

Fiona threw the sheet of paper on Barra's desk. 'It's not going to work. It's impossible to code up a single name for the computer. It's programmed for two names.'

'Yeah, I know. I'll have to write and tell him.'

Fiona sat at her desk and pulled a pile of files forward.

'Why would anyone want to be called Legs, for God's sake. I can understand someone wanting to change their name, but Legs . . .'

'Perhaps he's a leg man,' Barra winked suggestively. 'I suppose it sounds better than tits or boobs.'

'He must have a first name. We could code him up as something or other Legs.'

Fiona flipped open the top file. 'I'm busy; I can't waste my time with idiot letters.'

Barra said, 'Probably trying to be a smart arse. When the computer rejects and he doesn't get his cheque, it will be a different story.'

Belinda said, 'Why not just call him Mr Legs, then the computer will be happy and your leg man will get paid?'

'That's all right in theory,' Barra's greater experience made him patient and patronising. 'But what if we get another Mr Legs? Anyway, he could be trying to put one over us. No one could seriously want to change their name to Legs.'

'I suppose you're right – it's probably his way of getting back at us. But we'll still have the last say. We're the ones who decide whether to pay or not.'

'Yeah,' Barra sat down heavily, lit a cigarette and picked up a pen and wrote:

Dear Sir,

Your letter of the 16th inst. to hand.

I must inform you that this department cannot accept a single name as our computer is only programmed for a Christian (given) name and a surname. I would suggest you retain your former given name of Brian and future unemployment cheques be paid under the name of Brian Legs.

Your cheque for the period 2nd–16th will be paid in the name of Brian Legs. This arrangement will not continue beyond the 16th. Your confirmation is needed for future reference.

Yours etc.

'That should fix him, ' Barra said as he handed the letter to Megsy for typing.

But it didn't. Another letter came at the end of the week. This time the manager brought it to Barra.

'You seem to know about this – be a bit stronger this time Barra. We've got no time for writing joke letters. He'll just have to learn the system. After all, taxpayers' money.'

Barra hitched up his shorts and read.

Dear Sir,

Thank you for your recent letter regarding my change of name. I am amazed that modern technology has not seen fit to programme your computer to accept single names. Dare I suggest you should re-programme along these lines? But you may well suggest this is not my problem and of course, I would have to agree with you.

It was kind of you to pay me my last unemployment cheque in the name of Brian Legs, but as you point out this arrangement cannot continue. Nor do I wish it to. I do not want to be known as anything but Legs.

I do not wish to be known as Brian Legs. Brian is a name I detest. I even dislike writing it. It is a name without euphony or visual beauty for me. I do not want to be reminded in any way of the time when I answered to that name. I intend never to write or utter it again.

I consider the name Legs to be a name of strength and purpose. The word conjures up visions of striding towards a future, where one is dependent upon one's own ability. There is an historical significance about the word Legs, which is quite mind blowing if one is able to realise just what legs have done for man.

I hope you will be able to work out something with your computer.
Yours sincerely,
Legs.

Barra wrote,

Dear Legs,

Your letter of 27th to hand.

As pointed out to you in an earlier communication this department is unable to accept single names for computer programming. While being quite aware that you are at liberty to call yourself anything you like, you must realise it is the custom in this country for people to have a Christian name. The computer is programmed to this end and will continue to reject your claim for unemployment benefit as long as you do not have two names.

If you would like to discuss it further, you may ring or write to the above address.

Yours etc.

Barra picked up Legs' file and stamped it firmly, COMPUTER REJECT.

'I've no option really,' he told Fiona. 'I guess once his "regular pittance" is cut off, he'll stop wanking about being called Brian. He'll have to realise we've got guidelines to work by.'

'You don't have to convince me,' Fiona said, 'I think he's a nut case, though I must say, he doesn't sound dangerous; he's so polite.'

'He could appeal,' Belinda said.

'Shit, I bet he'll write another letter saying he's changed his mind. I told you he was a smart arse; talking about what legs have done for man.'

'Or a sex maniac,' Belinda said.

Legs wrote,

Dear B. for the manager,

I am intrigued you do not sign your name. Is it possible you also have a name you dislike? You may even bear the name I have renounced. Anyway, thank you for letting me know what to expect from your computer.

At the moment it is impossible for me to come and see or phone you as I am living in a tent in the bush. I have no transport and am dependent on the assistance of a passing car or truck to post this letter. I do not mention this to make you feel sorry for me but to explain my lack of presence in your office. As I have a good supply of flour, sugar, tea, rice, two boxes of bullets and a fishing line I will not starve. I may, of course, suffer from a vitamin deficiency through lack of fresh fruit and vegetables. I only mention my domestic circumstances so that you may be aware that I am not asking for any special treatment.

I have little knowledge of computers or, for that matter, any technology but I am at a loss to understand why you cannot communicate the difficulty of a one-name person to your computer. Would it be possible to fill in a couple of dots or even a few zeros in the vacant space? Do you think the computer would agree to this?

Yours sincerely,

Legs.

Barra went to the manager with Legs' letter.

'I think we may have to suspend his unemployment benefit. He's admitted he is not looking for work.'

The manager read the letter and looked thoughtful. 'Well, not exactly, though he has said he's going fishing and shooting. Send him a review form and see if his circumstances have changed in any way. We don't want to suspend him unless we really have to.'

Barra sent the review form and wrote,

Dear Legs,

Please fill in the review form for your unemployment benefit. From your last letter it appears you are making no effort to look for work. Under the conditions of the Social Service Act, you are obliged to be actively seeking work while receiving unemployment benefit. If you have not looked for work in the last fortnight, your benefit will be terminated.

Yours etc.

'In a way,' Barra said in the tea room, 'I've got quite fond of Legs. I almost look forward to his letters, if you know what I mean.'

Fiona looked up from the magazine she was studying. 'That's all very well because it's a sort of game, but what annoys me is the fact he is not keeping his part of the bargain. I mean, if someone chooses to live on a benefit, they've got to stick to the rules and the rules say you should have a first name. All that stuff he writes about is just a wank, probably because he's got plenty of time.'

'Perhaps he can't get a job,' Barra said.

'I don't believe that.' Fiona closed her magazine with a bang. 'He writes quite a good letter, so he must be well educated or at least fairly bright. A guy like that could easily get a job. He just doesn't want to – or perhaps he's a loony, which is more like it. Why don't you write to him and suggest he applies for an Invalid Pension; he might be able to get it on psychiatric grounds.'

Barra said, 'I'll wait until I get the review form back.'

The review form and Legs' reply arrived in a few days.

Dear B. for the manager, (Legs wrote)

Please find the review form enclosed. You will note my circumstances have not changed. I still live alone, I have no dependants, no job and no other income. I apply for jobs at irregular intervals, mainly because the type of work I am most suited to do is not readily available. As you may like to note on my file, I am engaged on a study of the impact of the man-made environment on the skink lizard (genus scincus). Although I make frequent enquiries and read the positions vacant columns in as many papers as I am able, I have so far been unsuccessful in obtaining work.

You may say that I should look for work in other areas. This is not as easy as it sounds. I live in the bush, as I mentioned before, have no transport which means it is difficult to find where the jobs are, especially since I have not received any money from your department for several weeks. A further handicap I suffer from is that I am inexperienced in other fields and although I have always expressed my desire to learn and to try any job, most employers want to employ someone who has done the job before. So you see my difficulty.

You did not mention in your last letter if you had been able to communicate successfully or otherwise with your computer over the problem of my name. I am sorry to have to mention this again, but my supplies are running out.

Sincerely,

Legs.

'This is certainly a knotty one,' the manager said after he'd read Legs' letter. 'I'll have to think about it. Just leave it with me. I'll get back to you.'

'I've read the manual and there is no mention of single names.' Barra bent down to tie his shoe lace. 'Do you think we should refer the file to Canberra?'

'Just leave it with me,' the manager soothed. 'I may have to consult the director. This is really a most unusual case.'

The following week another letter arrived from Legs. He wrote,

Dear B. for the manager,

I hate to worry you but really, I am becoming somewhat desperate. Two days ago I managed to obtain a couple of hours' work by digging a car out of a ditch. The driver had failed to negotiate a bend and had embedded the bonnet of his car in a muddy bank. As I happened to be passing, I returned to my camp and got a spade. After two hours of back breaking work, we were able to get the car out. Fortunately, the damage seemed minimal. The driver very kindly gave me $5 and a packet of cigarettes. I shall of course, declare this money on my next dole form.

I only mention this to show you the precarious state of my existence.

Since that time, I have spent the last two days near the bend with my spade, in case another car gets into similar difficulties.

Please give my regards to your computer.

Yours sincerely,

Legs.

'He sounds as if the whole thing has got to him,' Barra said to the manager.

'Do you think he is serious? I mean, funny things happen to men living alone, or so my wife tells me. I've never lived alone myself.' The manager walked to his filing cabinet and idly pulled out a file, looked at it and put it back.

'In a way, we can't not pay,' he said. 'I mean, he's really done everything we've asked him, except get a Christian name. He puts in the dole form every fortnight, on time, fills in the back and says he's looked for jobs. It's just the computer.'

'I suppose we could suggest he appeals.' Barra sat down and lit a cigarette.

'No, I don't want him to appeal; I've been getting complaints lately about the number of appeals coming from this office. It could be seen as not doing the job properly. Not making the right decisions.'

'Any complaints about a particular person?' Barra was casual. He took a long pull at his cigarette and ground it hard against the side of the metal waste bin. 'I'm due for my increment, when you write the report. I could do with the extra money.'

'Don't worry, Barra. If things go wrong, I'm the one who'll have to carry the can. That's what being the boss means.'

'I just wondered.'

The manager walked to the window and turned and faced Barra.

'Look Barra, you'll have to work it out. I don't care how you get around it, but do something and send him a cheque. A guy like this Legs could easily go to his member of parliament or even write to the Minister. Oh, I know he sounds very polite but he could really be dangerous. For all we know, he may have already written letters off to all sorts of people.'

'I could call him in for an interview.'

'No need for that; he's just filled in his review form and anyway, he'd probably ask to see the Director. I don't want that; I'm not too popular in that quarter at the moment.'

Barra walked back to his desk and opened Legs' file. He read carefully through it several times, lit a cigarette and pulled a sheet of paper towards him and wrote,

Dear Legs,

Your letters of 12th and 16th to hand.

Within the parameters of our guide lines, you appear to be eligible for unemployment benefit. The only criteria you have not filled relates to your name, as previously mentioned in correspondence to you.

As this department has no wish to penalise you, I have been instructed to find another name for you so that the computer will not reject your claim. As you do not appear to treat this matter with seriousness, I have no option but to find a name that is suitable to yourself and the department.

Would you consider being known as LEGS ONLY?

I would be grateful to hear from you as soon as possible so that you may be paid.

Yours faithfully, etc.

Legs wrote,

Dear B. for the manager,

I am delighted with your letter. Thank you so much for writing.

Contrary to what you say, I take this matter very seriously. Otherwise I should have agreed to be known by my previous Christian name. You may remember how I feel about it?

As to LEGS ONLY, I cannot believe you are serious. Do you realise that ONLY would then become my surname, with LEGS as my given name? The whole purpose of changing my name was to be known by one name; a name with no past and perhaps no future. A name which would stand alone, like a pair of legs, planted solidly and squarely upon the earth. Legs symbolise much more than skin, bone and tissue; they are my grasp upon reality, the world and indeed the universe. My legs translate into action the thoughts of my brain. They have become so sensitised, they are my feelings and emotions; the physical expression of me.

To be known as LEGS ONLY or even ONLY LEGS would negate how I feel about legs. So, I am not willing to compromise for your computer. This may sound inflexible but I'm sure you will realise how it is with me.

Legs is an O.K. name.

Give my kindest regards to the computer.

Legs.

'Christ,' Barra said to Fiona, 'what do I do now?'

Fiona was not interested. She'd arranged to have a perm at lunch time and was already dreaming of what Jim would say when he saw the glamour of her new curls. Maybe she'd have a rinse too; her hair was muddy looking and blonding would lighten it. As long as it wasn't too much, otherwise she might look a bit like a moll.

'I think he's mad, as I keep telling you. I've got work to do.'

Fiona dismissed Legs and Barra with a sharp opening of her drawer.

'Well, Legs' letters relieve the boredom a bit.' Barra picked up the letter and read it again. 'He's a funny sort of a guy; sometimes I think he's almost a comedian.'

He sat down heavily and chewed the end of his pen.

He wrote,

Dear Legs,

Your letter of the 30th inst. to hand.

Your comments re your name have been noted.

As this department has spent considerable time at the taxpayers' expense on your case in trying to help you to receive your entitlement under the Act, there is nothing further we are able to do for you, unless you agree to the criteria under which we operate.

Yours faithfully, etc.

Barra looked at the letter and with sudden resolution picked up his pen and wrote,

P.S. For Christ's sake, give me a break. What about OK LEGS?
Barra.

A final letter came from Legs a few days later. He wrote,

Dear Barra,

At last . . . you are a person; whether you are male or female is immaterial. You have a name. I know what B. stands for. You cannot imagine my relief at finding the bureaucracy is not just a machine like the nameless and all powerful computer, but is a living, breathing industry, employing people with names and lives of their own. You have restored my faith in the system.

How can I refuse what you ask? If I did, I should be refusing to co-operate with a fellow being, someone who, like me, signs only one name – Barra. I admit I am curious as to your choice but I respect your right to remain unexplained.

I am willing to be known as O.K. LEGS, as the initials O.K. agree with my philosophy regarding my name.

I look forward to receiving a cheque addressed this way. I am also pleased your computer will be satisfied.

Fraternally,

Legs.

Barra stamped the letter with the date and attached it to the file.

Teach Me to Dance

KERRYN GOLDSWORTHY   1988

'I loved him because he was a stranger. He was dark and different; he came from a foreign place, full of passion and history. . . He was a man, and a Greek; he was another country.'

An Adelaide high-school girl has friends from Greek and Anglo-Australian families in the 1960s, a time when 'new Australians' were expected to become completely assimilated into the British-Australian culture. The story ends with the captain of the cricket team behaving in a very unexpected and risky way at the school dance.

Kerryn Goldsworthy grew up in South Australia and was educated in Adelaide.

People from two different cultures also meet and learn from one another in 'Neighbours', page 3.

I saw *Zorba the Greek* at the Capri Cinema in 1967 when I was fourteen. Julie and I caught the bus to Helen's house and Helen's brother Chris drove us to the cinema and picked us up afterwards. My father and Julie's father had both said that if a boy was going to be driving us anywhere then we weren't allowed to go, but we told them that Mr Karipidis had said that if Chris *didn't* drive us then *Helen* wouldn't be allowed to go, and did they really want to be piggy like Greek fathers and have us grow up warped and twisted or what, and anyway Chris went to our brother school where he was a prefect (my father gave in) and the captain of the cricket team (Julie's father gave in). We didn't mention that we thought he was God.

In the dark, I fell in love with Alan Bates, and we all cried. At the end after everyone else had gone, Helen danced down the red carpet slope of the centre aisle in the dim light. Julie and I sat in our seats and watched. That was before I got my black dress.

For years after that film came to Adelaide, dances and socials and parties would end with everyone in a circle, doing Zorba's Dance. Kneecaps were kicked, at first, and people in high heels fell over. Later we all got quite good at it. At school there were a lot of Greek kids who had exotic names and brought amazing food to fetes: *baklava, kourabiethes, galataboureko*. They

In this picture the back of the Greek statue's head merges with the silhouette of a Grass Tree. These are a common sight in the Australian bush, with their tuft of grass-like leaves fanning out at the top of their trunk. They are sometimes called a 'Blackboy', because each has a tall, erect flower spike like an Aboriginal spear. They live for a very long time and grow very slowly – about one foot (30 cm) in 120 years!

From the Secret Life of Statues Series 1989, by Peter Lyssiotis.

taught us how to dance, we played Alan Bates to their Anthony Quinn.
('Teach me to dance . . . will you?' 'Did you say – *dance*? Come on, my boy!') I
had special lessons from Helen and knew a lot of fancy steps. She taught me
the Greek alphabet, she taught me how to tell fortunes in a coffee cup: a letter,
a journey, a troubled heart.

Over your thick school pantyhose and black lace-up shoes, and pants and bra
and petticoat and long-sleeved spencer, and white shirt and school tie, you
pulled the belt of your box-pleat tunic tight and bloused the top up over the
belt so that the pleats would fall straight on your hips and the hem would sit
level and short above your knees. If you didn't, the tunic bagged at the bum
and sagged down below the backs of your knees, and you looked like a dag.
You wore your school jumper two sizes too big and brand new, and in the
pocket of your blazer you carried a comb. You wore your beret at a specified
angle I think we all hoped was French.

You studied the pictures of Twiggy and worked out that where makeup
had once meant lipstick and rouge it now meant mascara and eyeshadow, and
anyway rouge was called blusher, as you kept reminding your mother. Hair
was like Mia Farrow's after she got it cut and they had to give Alison
McKenzie brain surgery in 'Peyton Place' to write her shorn head into the
script. You sang Eleanor Rigby and Scarborough Fair.

At school the idea was to get good marks, but not too good, and without
appearing to do any work. If you answered a lot of questions in class, or took
more interest in anything than the curriculum required, you were weird.
Either you were attractive or you weren't, and if you were you spent the
weekend doing your hair and talking to boys on the phone, and if you weren't
you spent it doing your homework and going for long walks, bopping down
the street with your transistor radio held up to your ear. Most of us walked
hundreds of miles that year, up and down, up and down, haunted by the
music of 1967 and wondering when everything would get better. We didn't
know what history was, or beauty, or the world. In class I sat next to a girl
called Anne Booker-Smith who spent hours drawing tidy maps of her future.
She would marry a boy from Saint Peter's College (a few miles from our
school) who would become a doctor and buy her a house in Unley Park (a few
miles from our school) and they would have two sons called Justin and Daniel
who would go to school at Saint Peter's College . . .

The most important thing about you was whether you were going out with anyone. That made you a star. If you had the chance to go out with any boy who didn't actually bring you out in a rash, you took it and were grateful. After a decent interval you dropped the boy, or he dropped you, and then after another decent interval you started, if you were lucky, going out with someone else. Those were the rules.

Two weeks after we saw *Zorba the Greek*, I forgot about Alan Bates when I fell in love with a boy called George Stanos. He looked at me over the top of his hamburger one winter afternoon in Waymouth Street and I was gone. I went out with George for five glorious weeks and got to kiss him and look at him a lot before I was dropped.

In twenty years of looking at men I have never yet seen anything as beautiful as George Stanos was in 1967. His hair was black, his skin was gold, his mouth curled slightly upwards at one corner in the ghost of a James Dean sneer, and whenever I walk down North Terrace I see the boy he was, lying in the sun on the grass in front of the War Memorial, propped up on one elbow looking at me, and behind him the great stone angel with the sword.

I loved him because he was a stranger. He was dark and different; he came from a foreign place, full of passion and history. And he made me think straight for the first time in my life about maleness, about the lures and riddles of a body that was nothing like my own. He was a man, and a Greek; he was another country.

Three weeks after I lost George there was a Junior Social at our brother school, and the social was my first real dance. Julie and I confessed to each other at afternoon recess on the Friday of the dance that we were scared and we did not want to go. We had a teacher who specialised in girl talk (the importance of personal freshness; the ethics of trying to get out of gym by saying that you had your period), a woman who spoke seven languages and had fled with her parents from Europe as a teenager in 1939. She wore her hair too long, we thought, for a woman in her forties – almost down to her *shoulders* – and she wore strange dresses of a kind we had never seen our mothers in. To our horror, she wept openly whenever she heard the word 'Hitler', and as she taught us German with quite a lot of history thrown in, the word 'Hitler' was sometimes hard to avoid. I now think that she was a beautiful and cultured woman, but we thought then that she was pushy, dowdy, hysterical and weird. We were afraid of her, and we didn't know why because we didn't know we were.

She had given us one of her intimate little talks about the dance. It was important, she said, that we should dress and behave in a way that was pretty and modest, like ladies. It was important that we should be at ease with boys and talk to them intelligently on the topics of the day. It was important that we should mix, and not cling to one partner for the whole evening. And so on.

Julie and I discussed this homily at recess. Neither of us felt like ladies. Neither of us felt pretty, or modest, at least not in the way *she* meant. Boys made us both sweat, as a rule, and though we both knew about the topics of the day we also knew that to talk intelligently about them to a boy was to invite a view of his retreating back. We snorted at the idea of an assortment of partners, because we were sure that nobody would ask us to dance at all. We feared exposure; we feared being branded as the sort of girls boys didn't want to dance with, which meant we would grow up to be the sort of women men didn't want to marry, and what would we do then?

Most of all, we fretted about what to wear. Julie had two possible dresses but couldn't choose between them: the blue one with the collar, or the grey one with the lace? I was still growing out of everything I owned and wanted something new, and I had already spent every afternoon after school for a week – now that my afternoons were free again – trying on dress after dress and then tearing it off in despair, sometimes with tears stinging the backs of my eyes: this one made my legs look like milk bottles and that one made my hair look like an army crewcut and one promising-looking red one turned my face a delicate pale green. I still didn't have anything to wear, and after school that day I headed back to the shops for a final, desperate search.

I nearly left the dress where it was. I'd never had a black dress before. My mother would say it was too old for me.

The dressing room was pink and smelled warmly of other women's bodies. I hung the dress on the peg and looked at it. It was black velvet with a white taffeta collar and cuffs and three small white buttons down the front of the short bodice. The sleeves had a big inverted pleat from the shoulder down the line of the arm, caught back tight and small again at the elbow by the wide pearly cuffs.

I took off the beret and the blazer, the new too-big jumper, the black lace-up shoes, the carefully belted tunic, the school tie, the white shirt and the long-sleeved spencer. I stood in my petticoat and pantyhose, looking in the mirror and hating it. No wonder George had fled, I thought; I looked like a bear cub whose mother had not yet licked it into shape. I took the black dress off the hanger and slipped it over my head.

One sunny winter afternoon many years later, when I had eaten nothing for two days and spoken no English for three weeks and was beginning to feel very strange, I turned a corner in the hall on the second floor of a *pensione* in Florence and saw at the end of the dim corridor, by a few stray beams of buttery light from the far window, a picture framed in scrolls of gilt and dust. In the half-dark I could see that it was the portrait of a woman, shadowy, still, remote; I saw the shape of her head, and her straight unsmiling gaze. An old picture, a person lifted out of time. I moved forward for a closer look and felt the fine hairs rising at the back of my neck as the woman in the picture moved with me. It was not a portrait, but a mirror.

It was only the second time in my life that I had seen myself clearly, with no despair or pleasure or relief, only interest, like meeting the eye of a stranger on a train. The first time was that Friday afternoon in the dressing room when I looked up into the mirror from zipping and straightening my black dress and saw that some time in the last thirty seconds I had become the person I would be for the rest of my life. I had hoped as we all do unreasonably and everywhere for a Cinderella-like transformation, to be a success at the dance, but this was something very different. The Prince did not advance in my vision; he retreated, right out of sight. Whether the boys at the dance would find me attractive in my new dress was not what I was thinking about as I looked into the mirror.

I was thinking I was free. The face of the girl in the mirror was neither pretty nor plain, but *there*, nudged into focus finally by a few yards of black velvet; on the Attractive Scale from one to ten she had somehow managed to disappear sideways off the graph, escape from the net of lines. She was telling me I had nothing now to fear or hope for from the dance; that I need draw none of the neat maps showing the doctor husband teaching Justin and Daniel how to be clean little snobs in Unley Park, for I would have no use for them; that I was free to wear my beret any way I wanted to and study as hard as I bloody well pleased. What I was not free of was my passion for George Stanos and for men who would come after him. But that had nothing to do with the graph, or the map, or the dance.

Ballroom dancing, like baggy tunics, unplucked eyebrows and very high marks in exams, was daggy. The school ran occasional dispirited classes in it from time to time, but to attend them was not a thing that you did. So at my first dance I was one of the two hundred kids who stumbled around on the slippery floor of the school hall in our best clothes, trying not to fall over, trying to pretend that moving rhythmically as you held on tight to a partner of the opposite sex, one you were right *up* against, *touching*, all the way down your *front*, was something we all did every day. We were the young in one another's arms, and we were hopeless.

I think we had all expected to walk onto the dance floor and glide about, that all the precise steps would come to us as naturally as breathing. We had been led to expect magic and ease, by movies and TV and fairy tales and songs and nineteenth-century fiction and old photographs of our parents, all dressed up at dances and looking pretty pleased about it and not anxious at all. I don't think it had ever occurred to any of us that Fred Astaire and Ginger Rogers had needed to rehearse. The cultural model for this kind of occasion was, say, a ballroom in nineteenth-century Paris where grown-up people, hung with emeralds and medals, spoke French and danced mazurkas under a constellation of shining chandeliers. We were two hundred fourteen-year-olds in a school hall with the chairs pushed back, with streamers and balloons in the school colours and a boy who was practising to be an electrician upstairs in the lighting booth; we were in a small city in post-Menzies Australia, the fag-end of those Edna Everage years that sent hundreds of artists of all kinds fleeing the country in boatloads, vowing never to return. And we couldn't dance.

George was there, avoiding me and my gaze. Julie was there, raising her eyebrows meaningfully at me over the shoulders of various boys as we shuffled past each other on the dance floor, and seeking me out in the breaks to compare notes. Helen, like most of the Greek girls, was not allowed to go to dances – not even to this one where her brother Chris was in charge of the whole affair.

Chris was in the First Eleven, the First Eighteen, the chess club and the debating team. He always got straight credits in all his exams, and that year he played the part of the Pirate King in a cherry-coloured silk handkerchief tied pirate-fashion round his head, with a cream velvet tail-coat and mushroom-pink knee breeches and high black boots and one gold earring, and when he first appeared on stage a lot of the younger mothers in the audience drew their breath in sharply and shifted in their seats. He was a flawless assimilator: he played Australian Rules, not soccer; he went out with

Australian girls; he sang Gilbert and Sullivan; he got all A's in English. Teachers admired him, mothers adored him, fathers wondered about him.

He was, I now see, walking a very thin line indeed. With a reputation like that he could not afford to fail one test, to drop one catch, to sing one off-key note. He was seventeen, and with three of his friends he ran the dance without once raising his voice. Kids who tried to sneak outside in couples were gently steered back in, and kids who'd smuggled in beer or Brandavino were spotted and quietly sent home. The four of them wore their full school uniforms with their prefects' ties, just so there would be no mistake about who they were and what they were there for. They were only three years older than us, but they looked grown up, and formal, and remote.

Nobody asked either me or Julie for the supper dance and so we descended on the food together, grateful for each other's company and for the chance to eat whatever we liked without being embarrassed. Anne Booker-Smith, who had had more than her share of some brandy that her snotty boyfriend from the school orchestra had managed to get past the prefects (she hadn't cracked a boyfriend from Saints yet, but she was working on it), dropped a piece of chocolate cake icing side down on Julie's pale grey dress and ran outside to be sick in the bushes. Andrew Carter, Julie reported, had dropped Robyn Donaldson just before the supper dance, and Robyn had cried. I replied that I knew for a fact that Sophie Lisgos and Dianne Martin were smoking in the girls' toilet, and that Kevin Boyle's new convent girlfriend had never had her hair cut in her whole life.

That was what the night was like, and that was fine with me. I loved gossip, and chocolate cake, and Julie, and I was still dazzled by the moment of enlightenment in the dressing room that afternoon: the event, the important thing, had already happened, hours before I arrived at the dance. I was sorry for the others, who looked as though they were still expecting it. But the lights came on and the band packed up and people began to drift out into the night, and still nobody had lost or found a glass slipper, danced in the moonlight, seen a stranger across a crowded room.

Then one of the boys who were packing up found a record that gave him an idea, and in a moment the first notes of Zorba's Dance brought those of us who were left back onto the dance floor for the slow opening steps. We put our arms across each other's shoulders and smiled, step-step-*kick*, step-step-step-*kick*-step, and the music went faster, and we got to the dangerous bit where you actually leave the ground, jumping and kicking, faster and faster, shouting and laughing, and ties came off and makeup ran and hair came loose from its combs and pins and Chris burst through the line of arms and into the middle of the ring, dancing with his shirt open, coatless and barefoot and shouting in Greek, calling his friends by their true names to come into the ring and dance. Someone went running up the stairs to switch off all the lights, and found Chris with the spotlight. Someone else turned the music up. Chris leapt and clapped and lunged and spun, alone in the golden spot, as though to deny all of his orderly skills and virtues, to throw off every fact about himself except that he was seventeen, and an athlete, and a Greek. One by one his friends joined in, throwing away coats and ties and shoes and flinging themselves into the light, four of them dancing not in decorous couples and measured steps but like men and friends and because they really couldn't help it, in a wild joyful way that belonged to another place.

Women, when we each recall our own first dance, are traditionally supposed to remember things about ourselves: our triumphs and humiliations, how we dressed up and did our hair, when we arrived and who our partners were and how we felt when we came home. And I remember those things. But what I remember best is that ring of golden light, with men in it, and beauty, and the rest of us a great circle of watchers in the dark.

One of My Best Friends

PETER GOLDSWORTHY 1982

'I know what they say. That violence begets violence, that a punch in the face is nothing compared to a hundred years of genocide . . . and maybe it's true. But it's also false – the blame's got to stop somewhere. Otherwise we'd *all* be guilty.'

The white narrator tells of his friendship with an Aboriginal boy in a country town, although his version might not give you the whole story of who is to be blamed for what happens. And is he to blame for what happens? Certainly it can take more than a generation to change racist attitudes, which the whites brought with them to Australia, but individuals and groups can help or hinder that process of change.

Peter Goldsworthy grew up in a country town in South Australia; he now works part time as a doctor and writes novels, poetry and short stories.

A different way of resolving conflicts between white and black Australians is suggested in 'We Like White-man Alright', p. 143.

People used to whisper that Willy had a touch of the tar-brush in him. That he was half boong.

I guess I should have known it was true – the accusation always drove him into a frenzy. And if I'd looked carefully enough, the evidence was there to convict him – the flattened nose, the brow jutting like a sun visor, the legs thin as spinifex. He had a good strong set of teeth, too – as abos were supposed to have in the days when they were treated like horses. Unreliable horses.

When I first met him, though, he was white. Or no colour – like the rest of us. As kids, we couldn't care less.

It was my first day at school – a day everyone remembers, but me more than most. My old man was in the Force, and forever being posted from town to town – so I had a lot of first days, in a lot of different schools. And being the son of a cop didn't make them any easier.

I always seemed to be wearing the wrong school uniform, or the wrong haircut. Or had a mouthful of the wrong slang. I'd arrive with a kitbag

Drinker, Tailor, Sold Yer, Failure, Butcher, Baker, Trouble Maker by Campfire Group (in collaboration with Michael Eather) Queensland.

BUTCHER   **BAKER**   **TROUBLE MAKER**

instead of a satchel, or a satchel instead of a shoulder-bag . . . Christ! I could fill a whole library with a catalogue of different school fashions.

And as I stood there among the stares and sniggers, the first to befriend me would always be the other loners. The dunces, the stammerers and stutterers, the fatsos – all the professional schoolyard victims. And I always befriended them in return at first, for they were useful to break the ice with. Although I often had to turn on them later as I settled in, and took my rightful place further up the pecking order.

Anyway, that's how it was with Willy that first morning. I guess he was just starved for human contact, and realised I wouldn't know who he was. Or what he was – an untouchable. He followed me around all that day – remembering it now, I could almost swear he was wagging a tail.

And of course, we were put at the same desk after the class filed in for the first lesson. There's a natural law about such things, a strange gravity that binds victims and bullies together.

It took a week or two to establish my position in the schoolyard hierarchy. A few bruises, a few bloodied noses, and a stage of equilibrium was reached. The bullies left me alone, and so did the victims.

Somehow though, I couldn't bring myself to jettison Willy. Maybe pity had something to do with it – there was certainly a lot about him that was pitiful. He could almost make me weep with stories about his life – the booze, the beatings, the foster homes, the good behaviour bonds. Even if half of it was bullshit, who could blame him for turning into such a miserable sneak. Any self-respecting social worker would have thrown herself on his flick-knife out of guilt. Or invited him home for a larceny, at the very least.

I remember one weekend we were out rabbiting – camped in the middle of a vast paddock somewhere. Just the two of us, and a thousand rabbit holes. We'd both got a bit pissed that night on a bottle of my old man's sherry I'd borrowed, and a bit giddy on his cigars, when Willy, for no reason, suddenly started to blubber. Snivelling about his parents, the police, the boys' home – the whole grim Fairy Tale.

'You're me only friend,' he whimpered. 'The only one who listens . . .'

Lucky for me, a trap went off just then, and the rabbit started whimpering too. It was Willy's turn to do the gutting, and when he got back I was asleep.

Or looked as if I was.

Still, I like to think I helped him. Hanging around with me, he learnt to stick up for himself more. Or maybe the other kids just left him alone more.

He was always around at our place on weekends, and would stay the night whenever my mother let him. And sometimes even when she didn't – I remember discovering him one morning curled up on the front porch. He'd been there all night – anything was better than returning to the home.

He used to come to tea every Friday night, and my old man would take us both to the Club – the Police Boys Club. That's where Willy first learnt to box – we spent a lot of time with our gloves on. My old man said he was a natural – all he needed was a bit more weight. We taught him to kick a football, too – and both of us played every week in the Police Boys team.

I guess it was one of the happiest times in his life – some recognition for his achievements, a bit of affection, growing self-confidence. My parents were even talking of legally adopting him, when he got pinched for illegal use, and sent up to the city for a year. Maybe he'd been too happy, and it blew some kind of fuse. As though he didn't somehow deserve it, or the guilt in him couldn't adjust.

'Once a boong, always a boong!' my old man said. He was really upset.

We were transferred again the next year, and though I wrote to the reform school Willy didn't answer. I knew he was ashamed of his kindergarten handwriting, and put it down to that. Then I settled into my new school, made new friends and new enemies, and slowly forgot about him. Although occasionally my old man jogged my memory with things he'd heard on the boxing grapevine. That Willy had left school, and was travelling the country shows with a fight troupe – and making a bit of a name for himself.

My life wandered on from weekend to weekend, through those endless adolescent days, those summers that seemed to last for ever. Then suddenly I found that I'd left school, and was married. A graduate from the Police Academy, being posted back to the same country towns I'd grown up in.

The inevitable transfer came just before my thirtieth birthday. We were reasonably settled where we were – a house and garden, a couple of kids – but it was worth an extra stripe to move. And I didn't plan on being a constable for ever.

Besides, I was curious to see the place.

I might never have left.

Country people never forget you – if only because they don't have a lot of other things to remember. But whatever the reason, they hadn't forgotten me. And I quickly found that I hadn't forgotten them.

The faces were all the same, if worn a little rougher with time. And life was still much as my parents had lived it – the same rounds of work, pub, and church. And footy on Saturdays, of course.

My wife liked to tell me I was too old for it at thirty – especially when the lawn needed mowing. She used to say there was nothing more pathetic than someone who wouldn't face up to their age. Maybe – but what I'd lost in speed, I made up for in enthusiasm. There was still nothing quite so releasing as putting foot to ball on a sunny afternoon. Or even on a wet one, for that matter.

And Willy must have felt the same – because that's where I first saw him again. He was playing for an abo team – the first year they'd had one in the local competition. The league didn't really want them – but some new discrimination law had been passed in the city, and they were stuck with them.

Not that the league was prejudiced – but every time the abos played people seemed to end up leaving the field by ambulance.

So maybe the league *was* prejudiced – against violence.

Of course, I didn't know all this that particular Saturday – no one had bothered to warn me. I guess it was part of the entertainment – see how long it takes the new guernsey to get his nose broken. And no doubt the fact I was a cop made it even more interesting.

I should have realised what was going on from the start. I'd never seen so many grudges settled, so much niggling behind the play, so many crippling tackles.

The first time I was felled, I put down to bad luck – but not the second. Or the third, or the fourth. Finally, half-strangled by a kick in the neck, I hit back. My old man used to say that abos have glass jaws, and the owner of this jaw was certainly an abo. He flipped over like a shot rabbit.

It was a crazy thing to do, but football does crazy things to you. I've heard TV experts arguing that team sports are a sort of safety valve, an emotional release – but that's bullshit. Football's where you *learn* aggro, not get rid of it. I didn't used to be a loudmouth, in fact I'm still not – except when I'm wearing a guernsey. Or driving my car, of course.

Anyway, as soon as I hit him, it was on for young and old. All over the field the boots were going in, the scores being settled. Something hit me from behind, I turned around, and next thing I knew I was squaring up to Willy. A whole crowd of the bastards was after my blood, but luckily some kind of chivalry seemed to operate – and he was first in line.

We recognised each other at the same time – after the first couple of punches. You never forget the combinations that hurt. He'd got blacker over the years, his nose flatter, and it came as a bit of a shock – I'd never thought of him as an abo. He was faster too, but after I'd stung him a couple of times he knew that whoever won, we were both going to be sore.

That's when he dropped his fists, and turned to the rest of the crowd.

'This bloke's a mate of mine – a good feller. Let's forget it, get on with the game.'

There were a few dissenting mutters, but Willy obviously had the authority – or the fists to back it up with.

I'd been forgiven, and that rush of affection reprieved victims feel for their persecutors welled up in me. I knew how lucky I'd been – there were bottles all around the ground just waiting to be broken and ground into my face. Suddenly I loved them all – Jesus, *nobody* knew their troubles like I did. Their brother.

I dropped my fists – and that's when Willy king-hit me.

I know what they say. That violence begets violence, that a punch in the face is nothing compared to a hundred years of genocide. That Willy didn't have a chance from the day he was born, that his options were nil in a world dedicated more to charity than equality. I heard all that from the social workers at the Police Academy and maybe it's true.

But it's also false – the blame's got to stop somewhere. Otherwise we'd *all* be guilty.

I used to think that people could be mended like any other machine. Pumped up with a little kindness like a flat tyre. But now I know better.

Every time I clean my lower plate, or my jaw aches in the cold, I know.

Black or white, Willy was a boong, and always will be.

Just like my old man said.

Paradise

MURRAY BAIL 1975

'The bus had PARADISE printed on the front.'

'Paradise could be close by. It felt close by.'

This story begins with a driver, Hector, steering his bus towards Paradise. (This is a real suburb in South Australia's capital city, Adelaide, where Murray Bail grew up.) By the end of the story, Hector has come a long way; and he at least is convinced that words make things real.

At the end of another story of a journey, 'Day Trip to Surfers', page 111, you are given various versions of the 'truth' of events.

Breaking into light, this long silver bus. It comes rumbling from its concrete pen. Grunting away. It reaches North Terrace by stopping and yawning; its full length swings.

Yawns left, climbs past Rosella, hesitates at Maid'n'Magpie, take the left, roads are empty, petrol stations are empty, car yards are empty, shops are empty, hold her steady, chassis doesn't pitch then, there are couples behind curtains, there's a dog, watch him, man on a bike, shiftworker in a coat probably. Now the road's stirring, milkman turns a corner, leaves the road open, driver taps the steering wheel rim, enormous view of life in the morning, foot taps contented by it.

The bus had PARADISE printed on the front, sides and back. It was a long run to the suburb. At the outer reaches it specialised in young married women with prams; and Merv Hector had to smile. From his position in the driving seat he could see the new generation hairdos, skirts, worried eyebrows. Gentle, slow-eyed Hector waited for them, was happy to be of service. When one of them waved between stops he could stop the great silver machine every time. His conductors were quick to see they were riding with a soft heart. Straightforward characters, they were quick to assert themselves. 'Be an angel, Merv. Stop at the shops there for some smokes.' They also went to him when sick of things.

This time his conductor was Ron. His voice, tightly pitched. 'Getting up at this hour really makes me wonder. We're not carrying a soul. Look, it really makes me sick.'

Merv shook his head. Through the pure windscreen the road was alive ahead of him. Below his feet the bus was really travelling. It made you feel alive.

'There's the people we get on the way back,' Merv said.

He made a long sentence of it, as he did when contented, and heard Ron's breath come out dissatisfied.

'There's too bloody many then. We should have two here serving then. All the school kids; they never have to pay properly. What time is it?'

They were entering Paradise. As usual Hector waited to be thrilled by it, he stared and was ready, but a disappointment spread like the morning shadows. Streets were golden but it seemed more like a finishing sunset than the beginning of a day. When he stopped the bus it seemed to be further away – Paradise did. New tiles pointing in the sky spoilt the purity. But Paradise could be close by. It felt close by. The air light, bright; he was at the edge of something. Hector's stubborn fifty-four year old eyesight produced these messages for his heart but he was required to turn the bus, and he turned the bus around.

'Hell, we're going to really get hot and crowded.'

It was Ron running his finger around his collar.

'She'll be right,' said Hector.

'Hang on a sec. Let us out at the shop. You want some chewy?'

Stopped. Merv Hector was milk cheese from Norwood. At the M.T.T. he was considered slow and forgetful. But he was dependable enough, and voiced no objections to the long early morning runs. His moon wife was stupefied by his sincerity. He was older. Their garden grew weeds. His watch was inaccurate, and he stumbled near the garden. 'Dear?' he sometimes said to Enid and faded out. The distance to Paradise, with the great screen framing all kinds of life, gave him this gentle advice: move, slow down, stop, let them get on, move, see, Paradise. The world was beautiful. It was plainly visible.

Now Ron said something again.

'Look at all the bloody kids. Just what I need. All right! Move down the back!'

The bus grew squatter and fatter with the weight of everybody. Ron battled through, and the air was hot and human. They were now channelled by houses near the city, yet it was confusing.

A green bread van turned while Merv wondered. The shape was smacked by the metal at Merv's feet and the whole green turned over and over like a dying insect, a round pole came zooming forward, Hector's world entered it and splintered. Glass splattered. A crying uniform over Hector's shoulder cracked the windscreen.

There was the crash, Hector remembered. And the memory of Paradise persisted. If there was a beautiful place he could watch for like that.

He was wrinkling and gave a twitch.

He found other work.

'Morning.'

'Morning. Six, thanks.'

'Six, and?'

'Eight.'

'Right there.'

'Two for me.'

'Back a bit, sir. Up we go.'

Inside a driver's uniform again. They hold their breaths and stare at lights blinking. 4,5, feel the altitude moving below the toes, 6, blink, blink, 7,8, turn the lever, doors further up: whrrp! abrupt stop, men breathe into ears, business face veins, Windsor knots left-right-centre. Right this little lift will help, reach the top, an essential task in the latest glass architecture.

I'll go to Heaven.

Merv Hector settled on his stool in the lift. Shuffling and throat-clearing squashed the space into a noise box. Like the run to Paradise, he was at the entrance with a mild face, helping them: they stepped out at certain vertical intervals, sped down horizontal tunnels for special meetings. These repetitions gave him the most gentle pleasure. He was in the centre of activity and happily assisting. His placid role in giving this regular service, regular service, settled his features.

In the morning a lemon-headed man unlocked the building and the lifts.

'How are you today?'

'What are you this early for?' the caretaker answered.

'Well,' Hector began.

The caretaker cut him off. 'If the others come here late, you've got to get here at this hour.'

'It's a good building you've got,' Hector suggested, in all seriousness.

'What's good about it? You don't have to live in it.'

And Hector had to take some keys to him one morning right up to the eighteenth floor. He was touched by the high silence. Outside the wind scratched at the glass. Inside currents of cold air tugged at his sleeve like the mysterious breathing of a giant snowman. It was some height, near the clouds. God. Hector marvelled. His veins, his eyes seemed to be swelling. Was this pleasure? It must be nearer to heaven, or Paradise, up there.

'What's your trouble?'

The caretaker came up behind.

'Give us the keys, and scoot. They're buzzing you.'

Merv ran back to the lift.

'Is it all right if I bring my lunch on the roof?' he called out.

'Christ Almighty!' the watchman said.

Why, the roof was high. It was peaceful. He could watch noises made by the street-people below. And clouds closed in; could almost touch him. And someone had placed pot plants along the edge, and wind trembled their green. Did the lonely caretaker put them there? The slow question gently surrounded him with pleasure, and near the clouds he chewed on Enid's sandwiches.

The lift was always crowded. He kept going up down, up down, all day. Now he preferred going up to down. Going down it was back to the street, hot and old. So he kept going up, and late one morning kept going, kept going, and wondering, crashed into the ceiling. Roof hit roof – or there were springs to stop him. But it was enough to jump him off the stool, and the caretaker arrived.

'No one's ever done that before, you bloody fool.'

'Strike,' said Hector.

He was dazed.

Merv Hector continued. His hour on the roof was something to look forward to. I'm very near it, he said in the silence. Full of pretty, dazed visions he slept past two, and was immediately fired by the caretaker.

'Even if you come here early,' said the caretaker, signalling up and down with his arm. 'Useless, useless.'

Hair on Hector's head looked electrocuted. It was fifty-four year old stuff flaking and greying: always looked as if he had left a speedboat. He wore brown eye-glasses. Sometimes he touched his lips with his fingers vibrating, exactly as though they played a mouth organ.

Home with Enid she carried on a bit.

But she noticed something. He had been weeding the garden. One finger was cut by a buried piece of china – a broken pre-war saucer of some description – and self-pity moved him to silence. He seemed to dry up. More or less alone, he shaved vaguely. He didn't say much.

He was not his cheery self, she said.

'Why don't you get another job, dear? We can settle down after.'

Hector agreed.

'You sit there,' the young man pointed. 'The phone goes, write down what they say. Just sit here. The Bureau rings about every half hour. Arrange the switches like so. You can make any words they tell you. At the moment it's RAIN DEVELOPING.'

Hector looked through the tiny window, looked across the wall of the building and there, in enormous lights, were the words RAIN DEVELOPING.

'If we had an automatic system,' the young man said, 'you wouldn't have to mess around with all these switches. But it's easy enough.'

'Yes,' admitted Hector absently.

So this is how the weather lights work, he thought.

This is what I do.

The room was tiny, concrete: enough to depress anybody. It was high in the dead part of the building, ignored by the air-conditioning. A plastic ashtray sat on the small table.

The black phone gave a sudden ring. A voice told him to change the message to rain. 'Right, then,' said Hector. He fiddled with switches, concentrating, then turned them on. Through the window he saw the sudden change in the message and automatically wondered what the people below thought. Would they believe in that? Would they notice his sign? How many would be caught without coats, umbrellas, rudimentary shelter?

But there was no rain – not a drop. Standing at the window he became concerned. Merv looked at his message. He looked down at the people shapes moving casually. Then, miraculously it seemed, rain began hitting and splashing. His sign shone in triumph; and the thought that his warning had saved people flooded him with specific pleasure. I was good, and he clenched himself. He looked up then at the clouds. They seemed to be pressing down on his room, around his life, down his mouth, showering his vision with rain. God, he wondered.

Down on the street depressed figures ran from point to point. The shining traffic remained queued, steam rose, and three silver buses waited bumper to bumper. It recalled certain mornings behind the steering wheel, the giant screen wipers scanned repetitiously like radar, squish-a-squish. Now he stared through the glass window, up at the clouds, up into the heart of the rain. He felt settled, sure, safe, glad to be there; he thought of home, the maroon chair, and his Enid.

Nothing's the matter, he said. I'm fine, he wanted everyone to know. On the panel he moved across and switched the message to FINE.

The huge bright lights said FINE as the rain kept splashing down. Altogether, Merv Hector marvelled at every single thing. He stared at his sign. It was true. He loved the clouds. It was another world, and he was there. The phone began to ring.

Enamel Plates, 1979, by Helen Lillecrapp-Fuller, born 1949, boxed assemblage
73 × 73.2 × 4.8 cm, Queensland University of Technology Art
Collection, Brisbane.

The Piece of Pork

MR TAN   1982

'What is that story all about? Why couldn't the poor boy have some meat?'

A story is something that is told by someone, to someone, at a particular time and place, for particular reasons. The tale told in this story originally came from China. It might become different when it is retold here by a Chinese man from Cambodia, now living in Australia, to an Australian woman, born in Scotland, who writes it down for refugees from Indo-China and others to read.

'The Larder', page 97, offers a sharp contrast to this story.

I would like to begin by telling you something about myself and how I was brought up. Then perhaps you will understand why, of all the stories I know, I have chosen to tell the one called 'The Piece of Pork'.

When I was small, my family was poor. My father died when I was only three, leaving my mother to support me and my one year old sister. To make matters worse, Mum was pregnant when Dad died and you can imagine how hard it must have been for her, trying to earn a living as best she could, and grieving all the time that the new baby would be born fatherless.

Mum went to work as a small trader, walking from house to house selling cloth. Fortunately, my father's aunt lived with us and she was able to look after my sister and me while Mum was out. No matter how she tried Mum couldn't earn enough to keep us properly. A few months after our new sister was born, my mother had to give her to relatives to bring up as their own. This meant that the baby would have a good home while we would have a better chance in life with one less mouth to feed. Mum could see her child often although the little girl grew up thinking of her as an aunt and not as her mother.

My parents emigrated to Cambodia from China hoping to better themselves in a new country but in fact it was a struggle just to live. If it had not been for the Chinese family system we would not have survived. It is a Chinese custom for relatives to help each other in time of need and in our case, my mother's second brother paid for our food and her first uncle gave us rooms to live in, in a building he owned in the Chinese section of Phnom Penh. The little money that my mother earned could then be spent on clothing and education.

When I was growing up I knew that we weren't well off but I didn't ever think of myself as poor. Certainly life was never dull. The Chinese quarter of Phnom Penh was a busy commercial district and full of life. We lived in a four-storey building which had a factory on the ground floor and rooms and apartments for families to rent upstairs. I played with the other children who lived in the building – in the corridors, up and down the stairs and sometimes even on the flat roof top. We never played in the streets – they were too narrow and too crowded with hawkers, streetsellers and passers-by. If we got tired of playing we could look down on the ever-changing street scenes from the balconies of our apartments.

Although I passed my days happily enough, I realise now that my mother and my great aunt, who helped to bring us up, must often have worried about what might become of us. Aunty must have been particularly concerned to prepare us for a future that might not be easy because she told my sister and me the story 'The Piece of Pork' over and over again. Hardly a day passed without us hearing this tale from her and because it was such a constant part of my childhood I will tell it here.

Once upon a time, in a very poor village in China, there lived a very poor family of just two people – a grandfather and his grandson. The old man and the boy, who lived together in a cramped hut, were all that were left of a large family. The rest had passed away from hunger and disease. Because the grandfather was old and not very well he could no longer work hard in the fields and had to earn his living by doing odd jobs. He could earn only a little now and again, so he and his grandson were among the worst-off people in the village, living on rice gruel and adding vegetables whenever they could afford them. Sometimes they went hungry for days at a time.

One day the boy saw his grandfather come home from the market with a big piece of pork. He was amazed because they only ate meat once or twice a year on special occasions and then only in very small quantities. 'Are we going to celebrate something, Grandad?' he asked. But the old man only replied, 'Maybe.'

Before lunch, the grandfather began to prepare the meat. But instead of slicing it for frying or steaming in the usual way, he covered the whole piece with salt as though he wanted to preserve it. Then he suspended it from the ceiling of the hut so that it hung directly over the table. Having done that, he cooked some rice and, when it was ready, he put bowls and chopsticks on the table and called his grandson to eat.

The boy took a mouthful of the plain, boiled rice, then looked up at the meat hanging out of reach above the table. His grandfather watched him, then said, 'Go on, have another piece. Doesn't it taste salty?' The poor boy looked at him in amazement. 'Go on, eat it,' said the grandfather again. 'Taste the salt.' 'How can I taste the salt when you don't even give me a small piece to eat, Grandfather?' asked the boy. 'If you think about it long enough, you will taste the salt,' replied the grandfather calmly as he finished his rice.

I was eight when Aunty first told me that story and I heard it hundreds of times without knowing what it meant. It was a strange story – the meat hanging there and the boy unable to touch it. It made you think. After a long, long time, when I was about ten, I finally asked, 'Aunty, what is that story all about? Why couldn't the poor boy have some meat?' And she explained to me. 'You're a child, but you must start to think about your future and what you are going to do in life. You must decide what you would like and work to get it. But if you can't get what you want, well then, you'll just have to dream about it.' And of course, that's what the child in the story was doing, eating rice but dreaming about the meat. He was learning to live with what was difficult to bear. He was learning to endure.

My great aunt brought that story with her from China to Cambodia. And a few years ago, before Cambodia fell, my uncle told me he had learnt the very same story from his grandfather in China. When I was in Thailand recently, I saw a Thai film and the story, 'The Piece of Pork', was told in it, so what was originally a Chinese folk-tale has taken root in Cambodia and Thailand.

Although I was brought up speaking Teichu, I cannot read or write Chinese. I was educated in the Cambodian language at a Cambodian school. A Chinese education was very expensive – the schools were private, fees were high, the uniforms and books were far from cheap. The Cambodian schools were government supported. All you needed were your pens and books and your mother could easily make the shorts and shirt that made up the simple uniform. You didn't even have to wear shoes. Besides, if you wanted to work outside the Chinese community, you needed Cambodian or another language, like French or English.

When people ask me, 'What are you?' I always answer, 'I'm a Chinese, born in Cambodia.' I feel Cambodia is my country, my motherland, but culturally, I'm a Chinese. And that is why I have told a Chinese story here.

The story 'The Piece of Pork' teaches that people have to learn to live without things they would dearly like to have. Many of us from Cambodia have had to live with the almost impossible – the loss of family, dear friends, home, country. I hope that in Australia, no one will ever have to experience the extremes that our parents and we have lived through.

Going Home
ARCHIE WELLER 1986

'Billy Woodward is coming home in all his might, in his shining armour.'

Archie Weller is an Aboriginal writer from Western Australia. In this story he explores what it means for Billy to go home to the Aboriginal reserve where he grew up, home from the city where he has succeeded in the whites' world as a successful Aboriginal painter and football star. The swearing in the Aboriginal characters' talk together is affectionately casual, but when whites confront them their language is deliberately offensive.

Other stories about friendship and violence in relations between black and white Australians are 'One of My Best Friends', page 35, and 'We Like White-man Alright', page 143.

I want to go home.
I want to go home.
Oh, Lord, I want to go home.

Charlie Pride moans from a cassette, and his voice slips out of the crack the window makes. Out into the world of magpies' soothing carols, and parrots' cheeky whistles, of descending darkness and spirits.

The man doesn't know that world. His is the world of the sleek new Kingswood that speeds down the never-ending highway.

At last he can walk this earth with pride, as his ancestors did many years before him. He had his first exhibition of paintings a month ago. They sold well, and with the proceeds he bought the car.

The slender black hands swing the shiny black wheel around a corner. Blackness forms a unison of power.

For five years he has worked hard and saved and sacrificed.

Now, on his twenty-first birthday, he is going home.

New car, new clothes, new life.

He plucks a cigarette from the packet beside him, and lights up.

His movements are elegant and delicate. His hair is well-groomed, and his clothes are clean.

In the Kimberley Ranges of Western Australia there are Aboriginal rock paintings of Wandjinas, like those on the left of this picture. Wandjinas, the spirit in the clouds, are both human in form – they have a head in the form of a skull – and cloud-like. Their halo-like headdresses represent clouds and lightning. Myths about these legendary beings tell how each Wandjina eventually died, leaving his image on the rock where it had been painted by himself or his companions. Aboriginal people believed it was their duty to maintain the paintings to show respect for these powerful beings.

Eternal Vigil, 1988, by Karen Casey, Australia, born 1956, linocut on paper, 30.6 × 29.1 cm, purchased from Admission funds, National Gallery of Victoria, Melbourne.

Billy Woodward is coming home in all his might, in his shining armour.

Sixteen years old. Last year at school.

His little brother Carlton and his cousin Rennie Davis, down beside the river, on that last night before he went to the college in Perth, when all three had had a goodbye drink, with their girls beside them.

Frogs croaking into the silent hot air and some animal blundering in the bullrushes on the other side of the gentle river. Moonlight on the ruffled water. Nasal voices whispering and giggling. The clink of beer bottles.

That year at college, with all its schoolwork, and learning, and discipline, and uniformity, he stood out alone in the football carnival.

Black hands grab the ball. Black feet kick the ball. Black hopes go soaring with the ball to the pasty white sky.

No one can stop him now. He forgets about the river of his Dreaming and the people of his blood and the girl in his heart.

The year when he was eighteen, he was picked by a top city team as a rover. This was the year that he played for the state, where he was voted best and fairest on the field.

That was a year to remember.

He never went out to the park at Guildford, so he never saw his people: his dark, silent staring people, his rowdy, brawling, drunk people.

He was white now.

Once, in the middle of the night, one of his uncles had crept around to the house he rented and fallen asleep on the verandah. A dirty pitiful carcass, encased in a black greatcoat that had smelt of stale drink and lonely, violent places. A withered black hand had clutched an almost-empty metho bottle.

In the morning, Billy had shouted at the old man and pushed him down the steps, where he stumbled and fell without pride. The old man had limped out of the creaking gate, not understanding.

The white neighbours, wakened by the noise, had peered out of their windows at the staggering old man stumbling down the street and the glowering youth muttering on the verandah. They had smirked in self-righteous knowledge.

Billy had moved on the next day.

William Jacob Woodward passed fifth year with flying colours. All the teachers were proud of him. He went to the West Australian Institute of Technology to further his painting, to gain fame that way as well.

He bought clean, bright clothes and cut off his long hair that all the camp girls had loved.

Billy Woodward was a handsome youth, with the features of his white grandfather and the quietness of his Aboriginal forebears. He stood tall and proud, with the sensitive lips of a dreamer and a faraway look in his serene amber eyes.

He went to the nightclubs regularly and lost his soul in the throbbing, writhing electrical music as the white tribe danced their corroboree to the good life.

He would sit alone at a darkened corner table, or with a painted-up white girl – but mostly alone. He would drink wine and look around the room at all the happy or desperate people.

He was walking home one night from a nightclub when a middle-aged Aboriginal woman stumbled out of a lane.

She grinned up at him like the Gorgon and her hands clutched at his body, like the lights from the nightclub.

'Billy! Ya Billy Woodward, unna?'

'Yes. What of it?' he snapped.

'Ya dunno me? I'm ya Aunty Rose, from down Koodup.'

She cackled then. Ugly, oh, so ugly. Yellow and red eyes and broken teeth and a long, crooked, white scar across her temple. Dirty grey hair all awry.

His people.

His eyes clouded over in revulsion. He shoved her away and walked off quickly.

He remembered her face for many days afterwards whenever he tried to paint a picture. He felt ashamed to be related to a thing like that. He was bitter that she was of his blood.

That was his life: painting pictures and playing football and pretending. But his people knew. They always knew.

In his latest game of football he had a young part-Aboriginal opponent who stared at him the whole game with large, scornful black eyes seeing right through him.

After the game, the boy's family picked him up in an old battered station wagon.

Billy, surrounded by all his white friends, saw them from afar off. He saw the children kicking an old football about with yells and shouts of laughter and two lanky boys slumping against the door yarning to their hero, and a buxom girl leaning out the window and an old couple in the back. The three boys, glancing up, spotted debonair Billy. Their smiles faded for an instant and they speared him with their proud black eyes.

So Billy was going home, because he had been reminded of home (with all its carefree joys) at that last match.

It's raining now. The shafts slant down from the sky, in the glare of the headlights. Night-time, when woodarchis come out to kill, leaving no tracks: as though they are cloud shadows passing over the sun.

Grotesque trees twist in the half-light. Black tortured figures, with shaggy heads and pleading arms. Ancestors crying for remembrance. Voices shriek or whisper in tired chants: tired from the countless warnings that have not been heeded.

They twirl around the man, like the lights of the city he knows. But he cannot understand these trees. They drag him onwards, even when he thinks of turning back and not going on to where he vowed he would never go again.

A shape, immovable and impressive as the tree it is under, steps into the road on the Koodup turnoff.

An Aboriginal man.

Billy slews to a halt, or he will run the man over.

Door opens.

Wind and rain and coloured man get in.

'Ta, mate. It's bloody cold 'ere,' the coloured man grates, then stares quizzically at Billy, with sharp black eyes. 'Nyoongah, are ya, mate?'

'Yes.'

The man sniffs noisily, and rubs a sleeve across his nose.

'Well, I'm Darcy Goodrich, any rate, bud.'

He holds out a calloused hand. Yellow-brown, blunt scarred fingers, dirty nails. A lifetime of sorrow is held between the fingers.

Billy takes it limply.

'I'm William Woodward.'

'Yeah?' Fathomless eyes scrutinise him again from behind the scraggly black hair that falls over his face.

'Ya goin' anywheres near Koodup, William?'

'Yes.'

'Goodoh. This is a nice car ya got 'ere. Ya must 'ave plen'y of boya, unna?'

Silence from Billy.

He would rather not have this cold, wet man beside him, reminding him.

He keeps his amber eyes on the lines of the road as they flash under his wheels.

White . . . white . . . white . . .

'Ya got a smoke, William?'

'Certainly. Help yourself.'

Black blunt fingers flick open his expensive cigarette case.

'Ya want one too, koordah?'

'Thanks.'

'Ya wouldn't be Teddy Woodward's boy, would ya, William?'

'Yes, that's right. How are Mum and Dad – and everyone?'

Suddenly he has to know all about his family and become lost in their sea of brownness.

Darcy's craggy face flickers at him in surprise, then turns, impassive again, to the rain-streaked window. He puffs on his cigarette quietly.

'What, ya don't know?' he says softly. 'Ya Dad was drinkin' metho. 'E was blind drunk, an' in the 'orrors, ya know? Well, this truck came out of nowhere when 'e was crossin' the road on a night like this. Never seen 'im. Never stopped or nothin'. Ya brother Carl found 'im next day an' there was nothin' no one could do then. That was a couple of years back now.'

Billy would have been nineteen then, at the peak of his football triumph. On one of those bright white nights, when he had celebrated his victories with wine and white women, Billy's father had been wiped off the face of his country – all alone.

He can remember his father as a small gentle man who was the best card cheat in the camp. He could make boats out of duck feathers and he and Carlton and Billy had had races by the muddy side of the waterhole, from where his people had come long ago, in the time of the beginning.

The lights of Koodup grin at him as he swings around a bend. Pinpricks of eyes, like a pack of foxes waiting for the blundering black rabbit.

'Tell ya what, buddy. Stop off at the hotel an' buy a carton of stubbies.'

'All right, Darcy.' Billy smiles and looks closely at the man for the first time. He desperately feels that he needs a friend as he goes back into the open mouth of his previous life. Darcy gives a gap-toothed grin.

'Bet ya can't wait to see ya people again.'

His people: ugly Aunty Rose, the metho-drinking Uncle, his dead forgotten father, his wild brother and cousin. Even this silent man. They are all his people.

He can never escape.

The car creeps in beside the red brick hotel.

The two Nyoongahs scurry through the rain and shadows and into the glare of the small hotel bar.

The barman is a long time coming, although the bar is almost empty. Just a few old cockies and young larrikins, right down the other end. Arrogant grey eyes stare at Billy. No feeling there at all.

'A carton of stubbies, please.'

'Only if you bastards drink it down at the camp. Constable told me you mob are drinking in town and just causing trouble.'

'We'll drink where we bloody like, thanks, mate.'

'Will you, you cheeky bastard?' The barman looks at Billy, in surprise. 'Well then, you're not gettin' nothin' from me. You can piss off, too, before I call the cops. They'll cool you down, you smart black bastard.'

Something hits Billy deep inside with such a force that it makes him want to clutch hold of the bar and spew up all his pride.

He is black and the barman is white, and nothing can ever change that.

All the time he had gulped in the wine and joy of the nightclubs and worn neat fashionable clothes and had white women admiring him, played the white man's game with more skill than most of the wadgulas and painted his country in white man colours to be gabbled over by the wadgulas: all this time he has ignored his mumbling, stumbling tribe and thought he was someone better.

Yet when it comes down to it all, he is just a black man.

Darcy sidles up to the fuming barman.

''Scuse me, Mr 'Owett, but William 'ere just come 'ome, see,' he whines like a beaten dog. 'We *will* be drinkin' in the camp, ya know.'

'Just come home, eh? What was he inside for?'

Billy bites his reply back so it stays in his stomach, hard and hurtful as a gallstone.

'Well all right, Darcy. I'll forget about it this time. Just keep your friend out of my hair.'

Good dog, Darcy. Have a bone, Darcy. Or will a carton of stubbies do?

Out into the rain again.

They drive away and turn down a track about a kilometre out of town.

Darcy tears off a bottle top, handing the bottle to Billy. He grins.

'Act stupid, buddy, an' ya go a lo—ong way in this town.'

Billy takes a long draught of the bitter golden liquid. It pours down his throat and into his mind like a shaft of amber sunlight after a gale. He lets his anger subside.

'What ya reckon, Darcy? I'm twenty-one today.'

Darcy thrusts out a hand, beaming.

'Tw'n'y-bloody-one, eh? 'Ow's it feel?'

'No different from yesterday.'

Billy clasps the offered hand firmly.

They laugh and clink bottles together in a toast, just as they reach the camp.

Dark and wet, with a howling wind. Rain beating upon the shapeless humpies. Trees thrash around the circle of the clearing in a violent rhythm of sorrow and anger, like great monsters dancing around a carcass.

Darcy indicates a hut clinging to the edge of the clearing.

'That's where ya mum lives.'

A rickety shape of nailed-down tin and sheets of iron. Two oatbags, sewn together, form a door. Floundering in a sea of tins and rags and parts of toys or cars. Mud everywhere.

Billy pulls up as close to the door as he can get. He had forgotten what his house really looked like.

'Come on, koordah. Come an' see ya ole mum. Ya might be lucky, too, an' catch ya brother.'

Billy can't say anything. He gets slowly out of the car while the dereliction looms up around him.

The rain pricks at him, feeling him over.

He is one of the brotherhood.

A mouth organ's reedy notes slip in and out between the rain. It is at once a profoundly sorrowful yet carefree tune that goes on and on.

Billy's fanfare home.

He follows Darcy, ducking under the bag door. He feels unsure and out of place and terribly alone.

There are six people: two old women, an ancient man, two youths and a young, shy, pregnant woman.

The youth nearest the door glances up with a blank yellowish face, suspicion embedded deep in his black eyes. His long black hair that falls over his shoulders in gentle curls is kept from his face by a red calico headband. Red for the desert sands whence his ancestors came, red for the blood spilt by his ancestors when the white tribe came. Red, the only bright thing in these drab surroundings.

The youth gives a faint smile at Darcy and the beer.

'G'day, Darcy. Siddown 'ere. 'Oo ya mate is?'

'Oo'd ya think, Carl, ya dopy prick? 'E's ya brother come 'ome.'

Carlton stares at Billy incredulously, then his smile widens a little and he stands up, extending a slim hand.

They shake hands and stare deep into each other's faces, smiling. Brown-black and brown-yellow. They let their happiness soak silently into each other.

Then his cousin Rennie, also tall and slender like a young boomer, with bushy red-tinged hair and eager grey eyes, shakes hands. He introduces Billy to his young woman, Phyllis, and reminds him who old China Groves and Florrie Waters (his mother's parents) are.

His mother sits silently at the scarred kitchen table. Her wrinkled brown face has been battered around, and one of her eyes is sightless. The other stares at her son with a bleak pride of her own.

From that womb I came, Billy thinks, like a flower from the ground or a fledgling from the nest. From out of the reserve I flew.

Where is beauty now?

He remembers his mother as a laughing brown woman, with long black hair in plaits, singing soft songs as she cleaned the house or cooked food. Now she is old and stupid in the mourning of her man.

'So ya came back after all. Ya couldn't come back for ya Dad's funeral, but – unna? Ya too good for us mob, I s'pose,' she whispers in a thin voice like the mouth organ before he even says hello, then turns her eyes back into her pain.

'It's my birthday, Mum. I wanted to see everybody. No one told me Dad was dead.'

Carlton looks up at Billy.

'I make out ya twenty-one, Billy.'

'Yes.'

'Well, shit, we just gotta 'ave a party.' Carlton half-smiles. 'We gotta get more drink, but,' he adds.

Carlton and Rennie drive off to town in Billy's car. When they leave, Billy feels unsure and alone. His mother just stares at him. Phyllis keeps her eyes glued on the mound of her womb and the grandparents crow to Darcy, camp talk he cannot understand.

The cousins burst through the door with a carton that Carlton drops on the table, then he turns to his brother. His smooth face holds the look of a small child who is about to show his father something he has achieved. His dark lips twitch as they try to keep from smiling.

''Appy birthday, Billy, ya ole cunt,' Carlton says, and produces a shining gold watch from the ragged pocket of his black jeans.

'It even works, Billy,' grins Rennie from beside his woman, so Darcy and China laugh.

The laughter swirls around the room like dead leaves from a tree.

They drink. They talk. Darcy goes home and the old people go to bed. His mother has not talked to Billy all night. In the morning he will buy her some pretty curtains for the windows and make a proper door and buy her the best dress in the shop.

They chew on the sweet cud of their past. The memories seep through Billy's skin so he isn't William Woodward the talented football player and artist, but Billy the wild, half-naked boy, with his shock of hair and carefree grin and a covey of girls fluttering around his honey body.

Here they are – all three together again, except now young Rennie is almost a father and Carlton has just come from three months' jail. And Billy? He is nowhere.

At last, Carlton yawns and stretches.

'I reckon I'll 'it that bed.' Punches his strong brother gently on the shoulder. 'See ya t'morrow, Billy, ole kid.' He smiles.

Billy camps beside the dying fire. He rolls himself into a bundle of ragged blankets on the floor and stares into the fire. In his mind he can hear his father droning away, telling legends that he half-remembered, and his mother softly singing hymns. Voices and memories and woodsmoke drift around him. He sleeps.

He wakes to the sound of magpies carolling in the still trees. Rolls up off the floor and rubs the sleep from his eyes. Gets up and stacks the blankets in a corner, then creeps out to the door.

Carlton's eyes peep out from the blankets on his bed.

'Where ya goin'?' he whispers.

'Just for a walk.'

'Catch ya up, Billy,' he smiles sleepily. With his headband off, his long hair falls every way.

Billy gives a salutation and ducks outside.

A watery sun struggles up over the hills and reflects in the orange puddles that dot the camp. Broken glass winks white, like the bones of dead animals.

Several children play with a drum, rolling it at each other and trying to balance on it. Several young men stand around looking at Billy's car. He nods at them and they nod back. Billy stumbles over to the ablution block: three bent and rusty showers and a toilet each for men and women. Names and slogans are scribbled on every available space. After washing away the staleness of the beer he heads for the waterhole, where memories of his father linger. He wants – a lot – to remember his father.

He squats there, watching the ripples the light rain makes on the serene green surface. The bird calls from the jumble of green-brown-black bush are sharp and clear, like the echoes of spirits calling to him.

He gets up and wanders back to the humpy. Smoke from fires wisps up into the grey sky.

Just as he slouches to the edge of the clearing, a police van noses its way through the mud and water and rubbish. A pale, hard, supercilious face peers out at him. The van stops.

'Hey, you! Come here!'

The people at the fires watch, from the corner of their eyes, as he idles over.

'That your car?'

Billy nods, staring at the heavy, blue-clothed sergeant. The driver growls, 'What's your name, and where'd you get the car?'

'I just told you it's my car. My name's William Jacob Woodward, if it's any business of yours,' Billy flares.

The sergeant's door opens with an ominous crack as he slowly gets out. He glances down at black Billy, who suddenly feels small and naked.

'You any relation to Carlton?'

'If you want to know – '

'I want to know, you black prick. I want to know everything about you.'

'Yeah, like where you were last night when the store was broken into, as soon as you come home causing trouble in the pub,' the driver snarls.

'I wasn't causing trouble, and I wasn't in any robbery. I like the way you come straight down here when there's trouble – '

'If you weren't in the robbery, what's this watch?' the sergeant rumbles triumphantly, and he grabs hold of Billy's hand that has marked so many beautiful marks and painted so many beautiful pictures for the wadgula people. He twists it up behind Billy's back and slams him against the blank blue side of the van. The golden watch dangles between the pink fingers, mocking the stunned man.

'Listen. I was here. You can ask my grandparents or Darcy Goodrich, even,' he moans. But inside he knows it is no good.

'Don't give me that, Woodward. You bastards stick together like flies on a dunny wall,' the driver sneers.

Nothing matters any more. Not the trees, flinging their scraggly arms wide in freedom. Not the people around their warm fires. Not the drizzle that drips down the back of his shirt onto his skin. Just this thickset, glowering man and the sleek oiled machine with POLICE stencilled on the sides neatly and indestructibly.

'You mongrel black bastard, I'm going to make you – and your fucking brother – jump. You could have killed old Peters last night,' the huge man hisses dangerously. Then the driver is beside him, glaring from behind his sunglasses.

'You Woodwards are all the same, thieving boongs. If you think you're such a fighter, beating up old men, you can have a go at the sarge here when we get back to the station.'

'Let's get the other one now, Morgan. Mrs Riley said there were two of them.'

He is shoved into the back, with a few jabs to hurry him on his way. Hunches miserably in the jolting iron belly as the van revs over to the humpy. Catches a glimpse of his new Kingswood standing in the filth. Darcy, a frightened Rennie and several others lean against it, watching with lifeless eyes. Billy returns their gaze with the look of a cornered dingo who does not understand how he was trapped yet who knows he is about to die. Catches a glimpse of his brother being pulled from the humpy, sad yet sullen, eyes downcast staring into the mud of his life – mud that no one can ever escape.

He is thrown into the back of the van.

The van starts up with a satisfied roar.

Carlton gives Billy a tired look as though he isn't even there, then gives his strange, faint smile.

'Welcome 'ome, brother,' he mutters.

After the Cut Out

D'ARCY NILAND 1987

'This was it. This was what he feared. Every one of them was the same, every country town.'

What frightens a 'gun shearer' (the best, fastest shearer in a team), when he returns to a country town after the shearing is finished on a sheep station? When the story opens, the gun shearer is in the pub buying drinks for 'the boys', hoping that these 'mates' can help him ward off that fear. This story asks questions about the strength of mateship – the loyalty and support men show to their men friends, which has long been valued as an Australian ideal.

D'Arcy Niland decided that to write about people he needed to live and work among them – which he did, as an opal miner, a circus hand and a woolshed rouseabout.

'The Three-legged Bitch', page 125, gives another view of mateship. And Bill Neidjie's story, page 143, presents a very different attitude to being out in the country.

He felt the first gnaw of fear about five. He had been drinking all the afternoon, shouting for all comers, drifting into their conversation, leaving them, drifting around the bar. Fat faces and thin, brown and blue eyes, teeth, lips, laughs in the throat and laughs from the belly, coming and going and gone.

Now the birl of sound was high. The pub was crowded. He wanted it to stay that way until the coming of the light, protection against the dark he saw deepening against the outside windows and through the door. He butted into a group and laid a note on the counter and cried genially to the barman to fill 'em up for the boys. He wanted their friendship, their comradeliness, their hospitality.

But the time was beating him and winning the battle. He heard the sound die down and as it did he swallowed with fear. He looked at the dwindling mob and his eyes were startled with something of terror. Hastily he barged about, seeking their companionship, inviting their fellowship, trying to perpetuate the social atmosphere and embracing it against his dread.

Then there was no sound. He was lolling over the bar. He felt the tap on his

Bea Maddock, Australia, born 1934, *Crossing the Square*, 1965, relief hardboard cut
on paper, 87.2 × 60.4 cm (composition).
Collection: National Gallery of Australia, Canberra.

shoulder: 'Come on, mate, fair go. We're closing now.'

He looked up like a fugitive, at the empty saloon, the battered face of the barman clutching a broom.

'What about you and me having a drink?' he cried.

'No thanks,' the barman said shortly. 'Be a sport, come on.'

The barman took his arm and he let himself be guided out through the door. The light inside vanished with the slam of the door, the grate of the key in the lock. There were still little groups about. He stumbled into them, slapping men on the back, saying desperately: 'How's she going, mate?' And: 'What's the time, cobber?' Or: 'Feel like a drink, just you and me?' They passed him off, and left him and then he was alone on the deserted pub corner, and the fear was solid in him and he felt stricken.

This was it. This was what he feared. Every one of them was the same, every country town. On the stroke of nightfall they became shells. Long, empty streets lined with still lights, lighting nothing except the shadowy, empty roadway and the few cars hulked against the kerbs. The shops were blind. Everybody had gone. Life had folded up. A great horror had driven the townspeople away, and in a while the grass would grow in the streets, the rust eat away the cars, and the lights burn on through the deserted day into the deserted night until they burned out: and gradually the blackness would creep over and engulf the town until it was a black ghost with no beacon to mark its whereabouts.

He looked about him with nervous apprehension and started off down the street. He heard his footfalls and they were like a drum calling attention to his presence. They kept the same tempo and the same loudness. Then the tempo changed and the loudness increased. He wondered why. Then it occurred to him that the extra loudness was not coming from his own footfalls. He stopped and looked quickly behind him. The deserted street stretched in dismal perspective. He walked again and looked swiftly, unexpectedly, around. There was no one in sight.

At the first side street he halted. He stood on the kerb. He looked down one way and saw the wall of darkness and the lights ballooning away in the distance. He heard footsteps, and his blood galloped. He turned casually around and peered down the street. Then to his right, in the darkness of a door-front, he saw the red point of a cigarette.

He walked across the street. He went along by the lifeless windows and glancing back saw a figure in an overcoat and smoking a cigarette behind him.

He slowed his pace. He felt the pace of the man behind him slow down. He stopped to look in the lighted window of a stationer's shop. He saw nothing there. Though he was ostensibly looking at the cards and pencils, calendars, books and figurines, his eyes were swivelled. They saw the overcoated man stop and look in the window.

He walked on, more quickly, and when he came to the Greek's he was breathing heavily. He sat down and ordered. The restaurant was empty. A plasticine Greek stood silently behind the counter with his arms folded. A mantel radio on a shelf was playing a Scottish medley. He waited in a sweat of fear, his back to the street.

The overcoated man came in and sat down at one of the tables opposite the cubicle he was in. The man took off his hat, put it under the chair. He put his elbows on the marble table-top, clasped his hands and rested his chin on them. The man in the cubicle tried to place him. He saw mouths and eyes and teeth. He thought he had seen him before in the pub. He remembered the hair but the nose was somebody else's. He knew the chin, but he couldn't remember the overcoat.

He jumped up and strode across to the table: 'You, what's your caper?'

The man looked up startled: 'Caper?'

'What are you following me for?'

The surprise turned to bewilderment: 'Following you? What's the matter with you, old chap? I'm not following you.'

'Keep away from me, that's all.' He said it savagely, fearfully, and turned quickly and went out into the night. He looked through the window. The startled puzzlement was still on the man's face. It relieved him.

He looked about him and went back down the street. He stopped in the darkness of an awning. He saw two men on the opposite side. Slowly they walked across. One of them was big, with a grubby white shirt open at the neck and swollen by his belly, the other was weedy, thin-faced and dressed in a sports suit.

He kept walking, but one of them called him: 'Hey, mate.'

He stopped, trembling, his fists clenched, sweat prickling his body. They came up to him.

'Got a match on you, pal?' the big man said.

'No, go to hell!'

He backed and broke into a run. The wind cut like a knife of ice against his face. It stung his eyes. His legs ached. His chest throbbed with pain. He had to slow up. He fell down in the long grass on the footpath. He heard them running, the light and the heavy. He put his arms about his head to cushion the kicks. Their feet galloped in a tattoo like kettledrums right up in mounting loudness to the threshold of his ears and he shut his eyes tight and screwed up his face. But there was no sound. There were no blows.

In consternation he looked up and about him. He was under the circle of radiance from the lone street light. He looked down the empty street. He heard shunting in the distance. There was nothing else.

Sobbing with exertion, he went down a lonely way, past a few silent houses with a light here and there in their windows. None of them belonged to him. They were all part of the town that had closed its doors to him and cast him off. He came back into the main street. He felt a wind rising, and it went with the emptiness and the eeriness.

He walked down towards the bottom end, and his footfalls unnerved him. They threw out echoes, betraying him. He sat down and took off his boots and carried them under his arms. He made no sound now. But the footfalls continued. He heard them. When he stopped, they stopped. When he started, they started. He looked ahead and behind him, and behind him he saw a figure step back into a dark door-front. He stared till his eyes watered. He saw it move again, just the vague drawing of darkness from darkness and the melting back again.

He walked quickly to the corner and turned it. He stopped. Cautiously, he peered around, but he couldn't see anything distinguishable, only movement in the patches of darkness.

'Hey, you!'

The sound jerked him around, and he saw idling towards him from the side street the weedy man and the big one.

'What's the big idea of – '

He didn't hear the rest. He ran straight down the main street, and he didn't stop till he reached the police station. The one word: POLICE stopped him. He waited till his shuddering breath came back. He stared back the way he had come. There was no sign of the big man and the weedy one, but there was the presence he felt was following him before he came on them again the second time.

It was blanketing itself in the darkness by the buildings, melting into the shop fronts and materialising. He half ran up the steps into the police station.

He burst out: 'Get them. They're after me. They're following me.'

The sergeant stared at him, the boots under his arm, his tortured face; and the young constable sitting back on the tilted chair put his newspaper down.

'Who's after you?'

'Out there. I dunno.'

'What have you done?'

'I've done nothing.'

'Talk sense, man. If somebody's after you they must be after you for something.'

'I've got a roll on me. That's what they're after. They want to do me in. You got to lock me up. You got to let me stay here.'

He saw the young constable look at the sergeant and he saw the return of that meaning look. The constable went outside into the street. He came back shaking his head.

'I tell you I saw them. I tell you – '

'Who are you?' snapped the sergeant over the words. 'What do you do? Where'd you come from?'

'I'm a shearer. I come in today from Moombala. We cut out there first run this morning.'

'Where are you going?'

'I got a pen at Glenman, and I'm off out there tomorrow. Look, you got to keep me here till then. Till the morning.'

'We can't keep you here. We'll be knocking off in a few minutes. Why don't you go to a hotel?'

'No! Worse, that is. I don't sleep, see.'

'You can leave your money here if you like.'

'I don't leave it anywhere. It's on me and it stays on me.' He trusted nobody.

'All right. I suggest you go to a hotel then. Tom, go out there with him and take him along to Savage's.'

He dragged on his boots, left them unlaced. He went along the way he had come with the young policeman who disdainfully said nothing. Every dark door-front he peered into held eyes watching him. They stopped in front of a hotel.

'Okay,' the policeman said, 'you'll be set now. Ring the bell and go in and get yourself a good night's sleep. Don't hit it so hard next time.'

He watched the policeman walk down the street and he wet his lips and tried to make up his mind whether or not to push the bell. He saw something move again in a patch of darkness and strained his eyes to identify it. But he couldn't. He turned suddenly and walked swiftly. His footfalls rang out. He half-ran. The clatter of his feet reverberated in the emptiness. He broke into a full run. He passed a lighted door, stopped and ran back and hurried inside.

It was a hall, packed with women of all ages seated on forms. There was a woman on the platform speaking . . . 'If women are to maintain the rights that have been won for them, if they are to uphold the social and moral sanctities and ensure that their children are . . .'

The words went into sound, all sound, pausy and highpitched, and he kept turning his head towards the door expectantly. He saw several women looking at him curiously. He didn't know what kind of club it was. He wasn't interested. He was glad of the light, the body of people. They gave him security. Then he heard clapping, and the women were standing up, and he realised the meeting was over. They began to disperse towards the door.

He stood in the entrance, watching them drift away, watching the hall empty. Desperately he stopped a young woman: 'Pardon me, lady, do you mind if I walk along with you?'

She looked alarmed, muttered something low in her throat and hurried away.

An elderly woman put her hand on his sleeve: 'Excuse me, are you ill?'

He grabbed at the concern on her face: 'Yes, I don't feel well. Not well at all. But I'll be all right when I get walking. Can I walk along with you?'

'Certainly.'

He stepped along beside her. He told her briefly he was a stranger; knew no one. He said he was broke. He thought hopefully that she might ask him into her place and they'd talk and maybe have a drink. Then he was silent.

They walked along in silence. He heard her footfalls, short, quick, beating between his own. His own trod on the top of hers. Hers were silent, then rushed in on his again. He looked straight ahead. He was just moving, the pavement clattering and thumping under him. He saw movement in the black wells of doorways, creeping elusively in the shadows, here, there, all about and about.

Then, suddenly, he was aware that the footfalls were not the same. His were, but the others had changed. They were not short and quick any longer. They were longer, softer, more measured. He knew them. He looked quickly to the person beside him. The woman was gone. In her place was the man in the overcoat. The man who had looked in the stationer's window, who had sat down in the restaurant, who had walked along behind him.

With a cry he pelted away, running madly. He stopped for an instant and looked back, and, fifty yards away, standing in the emptiness, was the woman in a pose of incredulity and amazement. Then he kept on running. He didn't know where. He kept going. His legs ached and the sap of power drained off leaving them rubber. His lungs sucked at whistling air. His chest was crushed and heaving with pain.

He stumbled and staggered. Then he stopped dead. His teeth chattered. The moon was thundering towards him. There was a hammering and a roaring in his ears. He stared, terrified. He shrieked in the hideous glare of the orb and fell senseless.

In the morning he found himself, damp and stiff, in the long grass by the railway line. He saw the station half a mile away. He heard the clop of hooves. He saw a yardman hosing the footpath in front of a hotel across the street. The sun crept warmly over the buildings of the waking town, and the shadows were all soft and warm. He checked his wallet.

Thank God that's over, he told himself. Next time I'll go home for sure between sheds, or go to the shed and stay there. No more of this coming into bloody bush towns with a roll for me.

He had said it before. He'd say it again.

And that's how Little George Orris, the gun shearer, came to be known in the outback as a bit of a hatter. Not that he cared.

Maralinga

LALLIE LENNON   1985

'. . . That could be poison you know – white fellas letting these things off.'

Lallie Lennon, a member of the Antikirinya people, has lived most of her life in the outback of South Australia, where her story is set. She tells of what happened to her and her family when the British were testing atom bombs there in the 1950s. (Students at Port Augusta High School helped to record the story as Lallie Lennon told it.)

Another oral tale of Aboriginal experiences in the outback after white colonisation is 'We Like White-man Alright', page 143.

I was married at the time with three children, and my husband, Stan, was doing fencing at Mabel Creek Station. We came down and it was a new Ghan running then – first time – used to be old steam engine – I came down on the steam engine – we was that pleased to get in this flash new Ghan – hiding our billy cans and all that – anyway kids were crying and we were trying to stop people looking – we was embarrassed I think – I was anyway – the billy can dropped out and we'd try to hide it. Banjo Walkington and his wife were on the train with us – she was carrying too I think.

We were going back to Mabel Creek. We got off at Kingoonya and got a ride with Mr Dingle, mail driver, he had all this petrol – right up high it was – forty-four gallon drums – some underneath and some on top – and I was big – just about to go in. Anyway had to climb all the way up there – got off the train and had to get on these drums – I don't think they cared about Aboriginal woman sitting on drums – he was only a boy, Mr Dingle – and I had to hold on to the kids – Stan wouldn't do it – they all sitting in the front there – and I'm holding on there – can't you hold this – asking Stan. Oh – shut up – he answers – anyway – I just had to put up with it and kids behinds was burnt with petrol – the petrol was leaking – mine was burnt with petrol – one place and I can't move with big stomach and trying to hold on to the kids – ropes – you know ropes was tied had to hold on to the drums – it was very cruel. Anyway we got to no. 7 and they said come in for a cup of tea Dingle – anyway – they went in – and one woman came out but I couldn't get down I

was stiff and everything – burnt – skin was burnt – petrol – and I was so wild
with Stan – anyway they got down and got their scones and that and cup of
tea – I had my cup of tea up top there with the kids.

Anyway we got started back to Mabel Creek – got off 12 o'clock in the
night I suppose – gee I was pleased to get off – so burnt with this petrol. Put
vaseline on ourselves and all – so wild with Stan – anyway we stayed there for
a while. We lived down the Creek – I was ready to go in – I said can't I go back
to Port Augusta – baby's ready – I shouldn't have went to Mabel Creek.
Anyway lived in the creek there – I thought oh well if I have the baby – if
anything happens it doesn't matter – no help see – anyway baby starts giving
me pain – that was '53 – anyway I went up the creek and had the baby myself –
cut the cord and that – kept it wrapped up like that. Stan never gave a cup of
water or anything – I just had to stay there – I thought Aboriginal women
have them like this – I might as well be like them – stayed there for a while and
Mavis brought some water and that – I had Jasol with me but I didn't have
water see.

That was when trucks was going through with these big things – didn't
know what that was – I was ready to go home then with the baby – and all
these big trucks going through – and all these people you know – dressed up –
uniforms – they were everywhere – I didn't know what was going on and they
had a big thing on top of a rise there and I was in camp then – dust was getting
on us from the trucks going through – Stan goes up on the station but never
comes back and tell me what it was – when I try to ask he says – Oh I dunno,
just trucks that's all. I just live along like that – anyway next minute this big
war tank went past – one – first time we saw it – guns sticking out you know –
was frightening – I thought – I wonder if they're going to kill us, I kept
thinking to myself – because I couldn't get anything anywhere. Oh they're
going that way doing tests on bombs – Mavis said – what Stan told her –
anyway stayed down the creek for a little while – Stan was walking around
with them – that was a long way from us – anyway they went on.

They said they're bombs. After that when they went up – a few days after –
they said bombs going to go off directly – Mavis said Stan told her they going
to let a test go and I said oh gee it's going to blow us up – I was scared – I said
well what's going to happen? Oh it's just going to go off – we'd better watch it
you know. I was frightened – getting up there and worrying about the kids –
what's going to happen – they'd be screaming – thinking you know. I
supposed they'd be screaming and thinking and running to me – I don't know.

Christ Speaks to the Women of Jerusalem by Miriam Stannage.
Collection: Art Gallery of Western Australia.

That was just going through my mind. Everybody else wasn't worried but I didn't know much see. Tried to ask Stan and it was nothing – so I just live along like that. I thought well if it goes off it goes off.

Anyway we were watching out for this – it was in the afternoon – must have been about 3 or 4 – we all watching you know and I was thinking I wonder if it's going to blow us up. It went off and a big rumble came on through – all right around – big noise – rumble – ground's shaking and everything. Anyway – saw this big mushroom thing go off and it just laid there you know in the sky – it was just like a white sky – like a cloud – you see a wide cloud just laying there – was just like that – next day when we got up that was gone.

Anyway after that I'm not sure if it was three that time. Two weeks after – that kind of thing – I'm mixed up with that one and the third one – I don't know whether we went back the third one or the second one – back to Mintabie. Anyway this bomb – they was talking about they was going to let another one off – I wasn't worried then because I knew it was going to go up like the other one. Anyway we went back to Mintabie for a holiday looking around for opals. June was only little. She might have been just starting to walk – I don't know so far back. Went back there and was looking around for opals.

We had our breakfast – got up early because we was anxious to look for opals. Had our breakfast. Bombs going up again this morning. Oh yeah. I was thinking long way from the bomb now. You know I wasn't so frightened. Oh yes it's going to go off this morning. We listen to the little wireless we carried around. We had our breakfast and washed up our things – put 'em all away and it's nearly time to go off now – we was watching out for it – made that same kind of noise only it was bit closer this time. It sounded a bit close but we couldn't see it – we was in a hollow – could only see the top of it. Little while after – didn't take long – suppose it'd be about 7 I suppose – you can see the smoke coming through the trees and the sky going – you know blowing – blowing through. It was sort of slow down the bottom coming but up the top it was sort of going fast. But oh gee, any way we could smell the gunpowder and Alec Woody was there with us and none of us were too sure. He said quick put the rag over your nose and he had a hanky over his nose – he was scared of it – was laughing.

Anyway at the same time I was looking around for this tree – it had sugar in it you know and I was going to suck it – like honey always runs down – I was

going to give it to the kids and Alec said don't touch that – it could be poison.
Lucky he did. That's when I noticed the dust was on the trees. Sort of a
grey/black, you know – not much – but you can see it on the trees – how it
settled. That could be poison he reckoned – don't touch 'em. Anyway I
wouldn't touch it – got frightened of it. It was only through him – I was a bit
scared – it was making me scared – that could be poison you know – white
fellas letting these things off. I never thought like that. And Stan said Ah! – he
was laughing – he went up on top of the hill trying to look for some opals. But
oh gee, anyway – it was that time – don't know what time the kids starting
getting sick – you know vomiting and rash and I thought they're getting flu –
forgot about the bomb – they must be getting flu again and I sort of felt sickish
you know and then kids were vomiting – all that. They had little bit of rash –
sort of a red – and I'd bath them in the water – we wasn't allowed to use too
much water – only one drum of water we had – and if the truck breaks down
we mightn't get water for weeks, so I just washed them in a dish and put their
same dirty clothes back on – it wasn't worth it – red dirt. Anyway – I said
these kids are getting sick and June was only little and she was sort of taking a
fit or something – jumping – I think she was overheated or something – too
hot – anyway we packed our things and came back to Mabel Creek –
Welbourne Hill. We came back and I was telling Joan how these kids was
sick. Anyway she said why don't you give them something – I gave them
castor oil before I came away because I only had a little bit in the bottle –
thought this'll clean their stomach out anyway – I thought – gave them that
and told Mrs Giles that they was sick and that and told her must be flu – bit of
a dry cough you know – I didn't feel too good neither.

Anyway she said, keep on taking the castor oil. She gave me another bottle
and she gave us – it's a brown stuff – you put two drops in the sugar – I know
the name of it – I can't say it. It's for cold or anything like that. Or if you have
a big cut you put that on – that brown stuff. It's not iodine – it's that other one
like iodine – pretty smell I reckon it's pretty smell. Friar's Balsam! Yeah –
that's what we were having all the time. Anyway we were travelling on to
Mabel Creek – I had dysentery – kids had dysentery – all sick – it was terrible.
Anyway we got there late so we camped in the creek and I was so sick with
this you know. I told Stan to get something from the station and they gave me
these white tablets to stop the dysentery – gave us some of that – take it four
times a day or something you know – couldn't understand anyhow – take
them anyhow. It helped. Jennifer wasn't too good at all – she was so sick. She

just sort of didn't know us – she was looking at herself – looking at her hand – looking at everyone's hand – she was sort of funny. I was worried. And June was taking fits. I had handful.

We wanted to go in Coober Pedy. Stan started growling – I don't know what you're running around for. I said there's no doctors there's no nothin' – I wanted help because station people – they don't help that much – didn't even come down and see us. That Mary Rankin she never come down and see what was wrong with us. Anyway I wasn't satisfied – I wanted to go in Coober Pedy. Stan took me in there – wasn't happy – but I was worried about the kids. We went in there and Mrs Brewster gave us cough mixture and said if they still take them turns bath them in mustard water – so I was doing that – mustard water – tablespoon full in this water. See I didn't know them people you see. Only she was a shopkeeper – Mrs Brewster. I don't know what she was she just told me to put them in the mustard bath and that's what I done and they were really sick.

I didn't know what to do – I thought oh well – just carry on look after them like that and then she gave us eucalyptus. If that brown stuff not making them any better give them eucalyptus in sugar – together – mix it up together and rub them all over with olive oil and eucalyptus – or don't give them eucalyptus – give them olive oil – plenty olive oil with this sugar – they just eat it – you know – they loved it. They couldn't eat much – just giving them milk and that you know – every time they have milk – bring it up you know. Jennifer was taking fits. June was taking fits. It was so hard for me. It must have been only a few days – no, a week after those tests.

We came right through in a Blitz. That's a big truck – an army truck – Stan had that – that was Stan's father's. Truck – old Blitz they called it and we had a little house on it – sort of like a tent on it and we had the tank under the campsheet too, tied around the drum – just get on the drum and up into the tent. We was living in that. Must have been a week they was sick. Think we only had one night from Mintabie, Welbourne Hill – then we had – I can't remember – I think we camped from Mintabie somewhere along the road there – next day we got to Welbourne Hill and from there we got to Mabel Creek and then Coober Pedy – and they were sick then all the time.

They were sort of weakish – I was sick myself – old woman was looking after two kids – old Toddy – she used to live in the dugout – so she helped me out with the kids – she took one – she's old lady, she was, and I didn't know her – a stranger but she helped me – she said I'll look after the baby while you look after the other ones – that was good help – and she used to rub them up and put them to bed. I was worried because she was in the dugout you know – inside – thought they might suffocate but they were okay. I used to go in and have a look – they used to go down the stairs and then go in like that. She helped me out. Barney was there with his mob but they were okay – it was only us who were sick.

I remember this bloke MacDougall he was trying to take the people away from Maralinga – shift them away – because he knew the tests – he didn't like it – he didn't like it at all – but they just done it. He was working hard; never used to preach or nothing. He went up there and he tried to tell them people and he couldn't understand their language and that kind of thing but he had a – he reckoned he had an old man there – he was talking to him – Maralinga – all around there – he was so tired trying to tell them people to keep away – big fire was coming he was trying to tell them – and they reckon the people – soon as he came away went back that way somewhere – telling the people to get going and them people went back and they never seen them people again – that's what I heard – Mr MacDougall was talking about it and Mr Bartlett was there. He was so tired poor thing – on his own. Had red – no had blond hair. Had fair skin and freckles – poor thing. He tried his best. He came back when everything was finished – he got all these people and took them to Woomera – we had to go and get our chests done and that. I think it was for TB that test. X-ray kind of thing. They never told us what it was for. I got this rash thing but they wouldn't tell me about it. I've still got that rash – go on until I die. On our heads too. I went down talking to them about it and they don't want to tell me. Tell me my father had it and my father *didn't* have it. We can't use soap – skin comes off. Bruce is bad, worse than I am. Bruce was outside with me – we both got the rash. Jennifer was playing with the baby inside the tent when that was happening – I had Bruce on my arm – watching.

There were other people around but we didn't mix with them. That Giles from Welbourne Hill, he died from cancer on his liver. Mrs Giles'd have a story to tell. The smoke went over them too. She was worrying about her orange trees. – Orange trees don't look too good. – Wonder if that smoke's doing that. After that again we went back. We're always going back that way because we were lonely. We didn't know it was dangerous – just thought it was bombs going off. Mr MacDougall use to help get injections for the kids – and Mr Bartlett – they were so good to the Aboriginal people – they were the only ones.

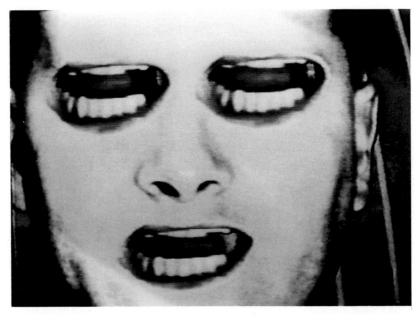

Details unknown. Frame from a DC TV Animation. Photocopied from 'Desk-top Video, Reasons and Means' by Tom Ellard, in *ARTLINK, Scan+*, vol. 4, 1993.

Just Like That

MICHAEL RICHARDS 1987

'The boy was amazed that so much power had come from something so small.'

It is sometimes said that non-Aboriginal Australians in the bush have followed this advice: 'If it moves, shoot it; if it stands still, chop it down.' In this story a father takes his young son out into the bush to shoot kangaroos, in order to teach him what it means to be a man. The boy learns another lesson, however.

Michael Richards is a photographer and film maker who lives in Queensland.

'The Larder', page 97, takes a look at some Australians dealing with off-shore creatures.

'Dead,' said the man, 'just like that.' He stopped the engine. The boy stared out the window. 'Well?' demanded the man. 'Do you think you can do it?' The boy said nothing. The man said, 'If you can't do it now you never will.'

'Yes,' said the boy, 'I can do it.'

'If you can't do it now you never will.' They left the car sprawled across the crest of the road. They walked into the paddock. The boy lagged.

'Don't walk behind me,' said the man.

The grass glistened in the early morning sun. The boy stretched hard to keep up. The wet grass was cold on his legs. Grass seeds stabbed through his socks and prickled his ankles. Flat seeds stuck to his skin. The soft hairs on his legs were soon matted and tangled with the sticky dew and the seeds from the grass.

The man stopped. He said, 'Watch.'

He raised his rifle. It cracked and the first kangaroo flipped into the air and fell down. The second kangaroo froze, staring directly at the man. He fired. The second kangaroo flipped and fell in the grass.

They walked to the bodies. The boy was slightly behind and on the man's left. As he walked his rifle wavered.

'Watch where you point that,' said the man.

The first kangaroo lay on its side with its head in a puddle of blood. Its forepaws were curled like small hands. It lifted its head to caress the boy with its large limpid eyes. He was surprised how peaceful it looked. The man squatted beside it. He poked its belly. He lifted its tail then dropped it so it fell like raw meat.

'Dead,' said the man. 'Dead below the neck. It doesn't feel a thing.'

The boy edged closer. He knelt to look for the hole where the bullet went in. The kangaroo swivelled its eyes, trying to watch both the man and the boy. Its throat was spongy with blood.

The man put the muzzle of his gun against the back of the kangaroo's head. The kangaroo jerked. Its lips drew back like a dog's. Then it was limp. Blood poured from its nostrils. The boy was fascinated. He had never seen anything like this before. He couldn't tear his eyes away from the bleeding head. The blood thickened quickly. The flow stopped. The man moved away but still the boy watched over the dead kangaroo.

It had happened so quickly and so easily that the boy couldn't believe it was real. He reached a hand to the kangaroo's breast. It was warm and very soft. The black eyes remained open. He couldn't believe it was dead.

He stretched a finger towards the coagulating blood but drew back without touching. The man finished the second kangaroo.

The boy asked, 'What do we do with them now?'

'Nothing,' said the man, 'let them rot.'

They walked further from the road, skirting thick patches of scrub. The boy felt very strong in the crisp morning air. He carried the rifle with ease. He enjoyed the strength of his legs as he strode through the grass. He felt that he could walk over anything that got in his way. The sun was warm on his face. They continued until they came close to the river, then turned and patrolled alongside the bank. Their wet legs glistened in the sun.

'Don't walk behind me,' said the man.

They entered a cathedral of great river gums. The sun filtered through green stained-glass leaves. The man stopped at the far side. He pointed. He said, 'If you can't do it now you never will.'

The boy swallowed. He cleared his throat. He swallowed again. He braced his legs wide and snuggled the rifle to his eye. He aimed over the head of the grey kangaroo. He held his breath. He lowered the sights onto the white patch of the kangaroo's throat. The kangaroo jumped in the air, flipped backwards, and fell. 'Great shot!' cried the man.

The boy was surprised how easy it had been. He couldn't remember pulling the trigger. The gun smell was sharp in his nose.

They found the crippled roo almost hidden in the grass. It was smaller than the boy had expected. It lay on its side, mouth open, breath gurgling deep in its throat. There was no blood. The boy stood over it, looked down, and felt nothing. He was empty as if his heart and his guts had been sucked out the barrel of his gun. The kangaroo twisted its head to look up. Its black eyes met his. He had never seen eyes so soft and so black. 'Kill it,' said the man.

The boy touched the rifle to the back of its skull. The roo stiffened. The boy thought it rattled but afterwards he couldn't be sure. Then it was limp. Its mouth and nostrils ran blood. 'Good,' said the man.

The boy was disappointed. He had expected more, but didn't know what. He had thought that somehow this would make him a man – but it had made no difference at all. A glint caught his eye. He retrieved the empty cartridge case. It was hot with the smell of the gun. The boy was amazed that so much power had come from something so small. He put it in his hip pocket. Then he stood up.

They followed the bank of the river. 'Don't walk behind me,' said the man.

They came to a large mob of browsing kangaroos. With their heads in the grass and their backs humped the roos looked like rounded red and grey rocks. The boy watched while the man aimed, not at the closest kangaroo, but at one that had lifted its head on the far side of the mob. He fired. The kangaroo spun and fell down. A grey raised its head like a periscope from the grass. The man shot it at once. The mob became restless. The man shot rapidly as the kangaroos began to move. They shuffled at first, not knowing which way to go, then leapt wildly in every direction. The air was full of flying kangaroos.

A few remained perfectly still.

Without meaning to, without knowing what he was doing the boy raised his rifle and shot the closest kangaroo. A small grey hopped towards him. He aimed into its chest and shot five times before it fell. Another raced across his front. He swung the rifle and the roo tumbled into the grass. He shot until his ammunition was spent.

Suddenly the roos were all gone. The boy was surprised to find himself with an empty gun in his hands. He pointed the empty gun towards the man.

'Don't ever do that,' said the man.

'It's empty.'

The man kicked the doe in the stomach. It didn't move. He kicked its head. 'Dead.'

The boy watched in silence. He watched while the man strolled among the cripples blessing each with his wand. The boy didn't move to assist. He waited while the man shot each kangaroo in the brain. Something inside the boy died.

The man rolled a cigarette. He stood aggressively with the rifle hanging loose in his arm. He gestured widely at the magnificent sky. He said, 'It's going to be a bloody good day.'

'Yes it is,' said the boy. He looked at the burning blue sky, then at the man. He tightened his grip on the gun.

The man blew smoke in the air.

The boy pulled grass seeds from his socks. Several had worked down inside his boots where he couldn't reach them. They scratched him each time he moved. 'Re-load,' said the man. 'We'll look for stragglers. Some of them won't have gone far.'

They crossed the flood plain, treading carefully on the uneven soil. The man was upright, his rifle in front of his body, his gaze levelled far ahead. The boy trudged with his head down, the rifle like lead in his hands.

'Don't walk behind me.'

They moved away from the river. There were no big trees here. The open grass of the plain was interspersed with outcrops of rock and patches of thick gidgee scrub. They trod a corridor between two patches of scrub.

The boy wasn't aware of aiming the rifle – nor did he hear the sound of the shot. The first kangaroo fell at once. The second bounded away. The boy waited. He knew it would stop to look back. When it did he shot it in the throat. 'Jesus you can shoot,' said the man.

The boy finished the stricken kangaroo the same way as before, while the man sat on a rock and rolled a smoke. Standing over the second corpse the boy sensed another presence. Hairs crawled on the back of his neck. He saw a huge buck on the far side of the clearing. It was the grandfather of all kangaroo. It glowed red gold in the sun. The boy was mesmerised by the big kangaroo. It was a magnificent beast. This one, this big one, the boy knew, would make him a man.

He planted his feet wide and braced himself firm as a tree. He aimed over the head of the big kangaroo. It was a very long way. The boy paused for some time watching the big red buck past the sights of the rifle and holding his breath. He lowered the rifle. He sighed. 'Shoot it,' said the man. The boy hesitated. He shuffled his feet. 'Shoot it.' The boy was entranced as the rifle raised itself in his hands. The sights dragged his eye to the kangaroo's throat. He fired. The big roo didn't flinch. The boy thought he had missed. He shot again. The big red didn't seem to hear the bullets go past. The boy shot again and again. The rifle clicked empty. At the same instant the big kangaroo crashed full length. It fell like a tree. The boy stared at the place it had been. It had been so far away. He stared stupidly across the clearing, the gun loose by his side. 'Re-load,' said the man.

The boy knelt in the wet grass. He laid the rifle over his knees and fumbled the magazine free. He choked it with cartridges, thumbing each down against the pressure of the spring until it locked under the turned metal lip of the magazine mouth. The magazine grew heavier with each shell. The spring tightened. His hands shook. They were slippery with sweat.

He clipped the magazine to the rifle. It felt as heavy and hard as a brick. He stood slowly. He didn't want to see the dead buck, but he followed the man. He watched the man's head. He noted the hollow above the collar where the man's spine joined the base of his skull. The boy raised the rifle. It was heavy in his hands.

'Don't walk behind me,' said the man.

The boy lowered the rifle. He joined the man by the great red kangaroo. Its throat had been pulverised by the slugs. The boy imagined it full of maggots, with goannas crawling inside it to eat out its guts. It would rot and dismember and its bones bleach and crack in the sun. The man kicked its face.

'Dead,' said the man. 'Just like that.'

The boy bit his lip. He flushed. Tears came to his eyes. A solitary crow barked far away.

The man turned his back. He started for the car. He said, 'That's enough for today.'

The boy raised his head. The world was blurred by his tears. He took a step after the man but staggered and almost fell. He paused to gain his balance.

The crow barked.

Suddenly the boy felt very calm. His eyes saw his hands lift the rifle. He felt nothing. He felt as if he were dead. The sights, blurred by his tears, danced about the man's head. They steadied a moment. 'Dead,' said the boy.

Bus Stop 1988 by Noel McKenna.

Bill Sprockett's Land

ELIZABETH JOLLEY 1976

'After every dreary week in the factory and the boarding house he went out to look at the land and every Sunday he wrote to his father telling him everything that was being done.'

Australia's wide open spaces have encouraged many immigrants, like Bill Sprockett and his father from England, to dream of owning land and a house of their own. Dreams can become real to those who dream them; or reality can reveal dreams are merely dreams.

As a young woman Elizabeth Jolley came out from England to Western Australia, where she has a small goose farm and orchard and writes novels and short stories.

'Warrigal', page 101, offers a different view of the suburban dream, from the other side of the fence.

Every time Bill Sprockett left the wooden verandah of the lodging house, 'ADASTRA' *Superior Board Residence for Men*, and went for the bus to go out to the hills, he felt a happiness and a sadness which was hard to put into words of any kind. It was a relief to leave the smell of cheap meat stewing and the shrill scolding voice of his landlady.

'I'm like a scalded bat outa hell this morning,' this was her daily hymn. 'I'll never get done in a month of Sundays. All these dishes to do, and just look at your room Mr Sprockett! Mr William Sprockett just take a look at all that dust!'

Symbols of his dreary existence. The room had so little in it that it could hardly be accused of untidiness, but the old floor boards exuded from their splintery cracks indescribable dirt and fluff. It seemed to crawl out all the time, especially at night, and lay in unsightly tufts, guilty and obscene in the slow warm shafts of morning sunshine, the only beautiful thing the room had, and that was gone of course when he came home after a weary futile day at the vegetable processing factory where he worked.

Every weekend when other people were trimming their lawns or watching sport, Bill Sprockett went out to the country to look at his land. He took the bus to the Kalamount Hotel and walked on up the hill from there. The road was newly made, the edges, turned up and heaped aside by some big machine, were like little cliffs of crumbling red earth, stuck all over with the burnt stumps of half-uprooted blackboys and toppling crazy bushes of the prickly moses. Back a bit from the road the wild hovea, growing in clumps, clambered over the undergrowth and hung down in curtains of misty blue flowers.

He left the road and walked in the scrub to the top of the rise to a place where he could look down across the sun-warmed slopes. The tops of the trees caressed the middle distance between the earth and the sky and every time he felt as if he was seeing the land for the first time. Every time he had the feeling that he was the first person to look down this valley, for the first time. Across the stillness the air was soft and fragrant and echoing with the sound of frogs croaking. He had never known before such a stillness and such a peacefulness.

The land was marked off in lots, little wooden stakes with numbers on them were stuck fast in the soil. It was all for sale right down and along this valley. Here and there dead trees held out their broken arms and stood headless, haunting the grey green growth of the bush with their ghostlike whiteness. The peaceful stillness was unbelievable.

The valley was being sold, some of it could have been his land but he had no money to buy any.

Then his father sent him a cheque. It was the savings of years and the amount seemed unreal.

'Your mother's had a stroke,' his father wrote and went on to say that because of this they would not be able to come out to Western Australia to Bill as they had planned. 'Buy some land Billy,' his father wrote, 'and tell us how you get on.'

Bill Sprockett meant to do as his father said and he went every week, on Saturdays, to look at this valley. And in the evenings, because he was lonely, he went to the trots and he spent just a little of the money. He always lost the money and every week, his face glowing and relaxed after the day in the fresh air, he tried again and again to retrieve what he had lost. But always his luck was bad and the money dwindled hopelessly, and his life went on week after week, dreary and futile and lonely as before.

But he had already written to his father describing the land, the beautiful gentle slope of it and the length of time the sun lay upon this slope and the way the wind blew softly there, gentle caressing wind, never a gale. And the creek was never dry, never even in the hottest summer, a waterfall fell down the rocky boundary, and all the year round the rocks shone silver in the sunlight with the streak of precious water.

And his father wrote back to say it sounded all right and he was glad there was water there and he was looking forward to hearing more about it.

So Bill went out as usual on Saturday, on the bus, and walked up and looked down the valley and watched the man, whose land it now was, begin the clearing of it. And on the Sunday he sat in his ugly little room and wrote to his father describing the men working and the machine they had for uprooting the dead trees and tearing up the scrub. It seemed as if the soil was bleeding, he wrote, it showed so red in the late afternoon sunshine. And he wrote about the burning in the evening, the smoke curling up and the hillsides aglow with so many smouldering fires.

After every dreary week in the factory and the boarding house he went out to look at the land and every Sunday he wrote to his father telling him everything that was being done. There were the foundations and then the building of the house and then the outhouses, and the installing of two sparkling galvanised water tanks. Then there was the preparation of the garden and the orchards. Every week there was something else to write about.

There was a brown-haired woman he could see there and he wrote about her, Peggy he called her, and his father straight away sent a letter back to say how glad he was Bill was settling down at last.

The curtains went up in the little windows.

'The curtains are white,' Bill wrote, 'and the front door is going to be red when it's finished.'

The weeks and months went by and there was a cot, draped in green gauze, on the porch by the back door and Bill wrote to say that the orchards were coming along nicely and the baby was fine.

Soon there was another little baby kicking and crying in the cot and the first one, now a fair-haired little girl, was toddling about all over the garden.

'You should see her on her tricycle!' Bill wrote, sitting in his lonely shabby depressing room. 'You should just see her get up and down the path on it! and the trees are bearing.'

Every time he went up to his quiet place among the trees above the valley to look upon it, he marvelled at the progress he could see. Sadly every week he enjoyed going there.

Being a landowner, even if only in his dreams and in his watching, he found he had worries and difficulties. One year there were very bad bush fires, and his father reading about them in his English newspaper, wrote anxiously. And Bill was obliged to take a sickie from the factory in the middle of the week to go out there as quickly as he could. There was such a danger from the long grass and dry scrub, tinder in the hot sun, on other people's neglected land, he wrote to his father in the evening, but all was well, the valley fortunately had not been in the path of the fire. And he wrote an extra page describing how everyone worked to prevent the fires from spreading, he wrote about their equipment and how, in the evenings, there was a queue of tired men waiting to have treatment for their scorched, incredibly painful, sore eyes.

And so the years went by and then Bill's mother, paralysed and bedridden this long time in the small front bedroom of the small house in the Black Country, died. And Fred Sprockett, sitting on a box in the damp aromatic warmth of his greenhouse, wrote to Bill in his careful but shaky handwriting. There was nothing to keep him in England now, he wrote, and he had been saving up and he was coming out. He had the fare, every penny of it, and he was coming out to see the realisation of his dream at long last.

At the place of look-out on the rise between the thin eucalypts and the quaint twisted banksias the old man leaned eagerly forward. His eyes were bright with happiness as he looked down the sun-warmed slope where the trees reached their narrow glittering leaves up towards the sky, and beyond these trees to the clearing where the neat brick house stood. The windows sparkled and clean washing flapped lazily on the modern aluminium hoist. He could see the lemon tree by the back door and the white hens down at the end of the garden. There was a rooster too, they could hear him now and then even from this distance. There was such a peacefulness and a quietness and sounds seemed to carry clearly.

'Hark at them pullets talking!' the old man said, not hiding his delight at all.

Bill Sprockett could hardly bear to look at his father. He had forgotten to count the years going by and the old man's aged frailness had shocked him when he went to the ship. He was glad he had hired a car to fetch him. They had come straight out to this place.

The work of all the years lay before them, serene and safe and comfortable, with more than a suggestion of prosperity, in the tranquil sunshine. It was all enhanced by the love shining softly from the old man's eyes.

The two fair-haired girls, now quite grown, were standing near the gate, they were surrounded by flowers, roses and pinks and geraniums and marigolds, a mass of colour. And behind the house, the compact little trees of the orange groves ran in neat ribs, radiating from the side and the end of the garden, down the slope of the valley. The fruit shone like little round golden lamps in the dark glossy leaves. Edging the orchard were plum and peach trees, purple and pink blossom lay along their slender branches.

'I've dreamed about this all these years,' the old man said.

Bill was looking down at the place too, it was the last time he would be coming to look. He hardly saw the prettiness.

If only his father could die now, at this moment. He was old enough to die. Most old men didn't live this long. Eighty-seven was a good age, too old to be changing your way of life surely. And too old to have to bear such a disappointment. It wasn't that he wished death for the old man. He never had felt like this before in his life, he had never known or even thought before as he was thinking now: it was a deep love for his father he felt and he knew he couldn't bear to tell him the truth about the land.

However could he tell him.

'Shall we go down now?' the old man asked. He was wondering about his daughter-in-law. He had dressed himself neatly in his best clothes for her.

'I hope she takes to me, and them girls too! Let's go down,' he said.

The sight of the old man's new boots irritated Bill and touched him at the same time, he felt an indescribable pain as he looked at his father's boots.

'I've been dreaming too,' he said suddenly in a voice which was quite unlike his own. 'I have to tell you something, Dad,' he began, and his harsh voice trembled and crumbled.

The old man looked at him not understanding what was wrong at first, and then slowly he began to understand. And it was in a moment of deep agony he understood his son for the first time in over forty years. His disappointment was such that he felt he could not bear it, not for himself, what did an old man like him matter, but for his son. He wished for words to offer the love and pity he felt.

They did not look down to the place again, of course it was nothing to them. Without meaning to, in their shame, they crushed little flowers, little clusters of coral and tiny exquisite orchids with their boots as they slowly made their way back through the scrub to the hired car, the prolonged melancholy crow of the rooster following across the deceptive distance.

And Bill Sprockett wondered if he could ask his landlady for a room with linoleum for his father.

Telling Tales

ZENY GILES 1988

'Women want power,' says Mikhali, 'and they will not be satisfied until they hold it in their hands.'

Zeny Giles was born in Sydney; her father was Cypriot and her mother Greek.

Within this story there are other stories, told by Greek men. Two women listen; one is from Greece, the other is born in Australia of Greek parents. At the end, whose point of view wins out?

'The Piece of Pork', page 49, is another story that dwells on the traditions that people have brought with them to Australia.

Mikhali, his brother-in-law Pericles and his daughter the teacher, sit on deck chairs near the Olympic Pool eating the last of their chocolate hearts. Since Mikhali's wife has gone back to the motel to rest, he and his brother-in-law have become unusually talkative.

'Do you know what they do,' Mikhali complains to his daughter. 'They line up at the Baths at six thirty.'

'But if they get here first Dad . . .'

'Listen, listen while I tell you,' he interrupts. 'They pay their money, they go inside, they take their towels and the towels of their friends – one, two, three – sometimes four, and hang them over the doors of the cabins.'

'And they are all the sunny ones,' confirms Pericles. 'We haven't had a cabin in the sun since we arrived here a week ago.'

'And I'll tell you what else they do,' says Mikhali. 'See that tall bossy one over there holding the blue towel. She ordered me out of the place because it was time for the women to swim alone. But I got back at her the next day. I said to her, "You see how crowded we are in the mixed pool, why don't you go now to the pool where the women are swimming alone?"'

His daughter is surprised to hear him confronting strangers in this way.

'And there are women who stand too long in front of the spurting water,' says Pericles. 'Three minutes it says on the signs and then another should come.'

'Perhaps they don't read English, Theo Pericles,' she says to her usually gentle uncle.

'Surely one of their compatriots can tell them,' says Pericles speaking with even more feeling. 'They stand, they swim, they drink, while the rest of us wait. They want too much.'

'That's right,' says Mikhali. 'The women want too much.'

She knows as she listens to her father that he is thinking not only of the women in the pool, but of her mother, his wife, who in her sixties has insisted on a bank account of her own.

'But they will wreck things for themselves – especially the young ones. What man wants to marry today when the girls give them everything?'

Pericles nods, thinking of his own son, almost thirty and still unmarried.

Another Greek, a man from Samos in his middle fifties, pulls over his deck chair and joins in the discussion. 'You're right, compatriot. And I can tell you that if I had what the young men get today, I would never have thought of marrying.' He puts down his belongings on a nearby table, offers his cigarettes to the others, then lights one for himself.

'And if they do marry,' says Mikhali, 'how can they stay married? As soon as there's a fight, they decide to split up. Nobody needs anybody any more. The women earn as much as the men.'

'Do you see how these women fight to get the higher wages?' says the man from Samos.

The woman sits back and watches them. She is Australian-born. Her spoken Greek is not fluent but she can follow their conversation and she continues to be amazed by their list of grievances and the vigour of their resentment.

'Women want power,' says Mikhali, 'and they will not be satisfied until they hold it in their hands. You know the story of the king who loved his wife and wanted to give her a special gift?'

The men move their chairs closer. Mikhali's daughter leaves hers where it is, but listens carefully.

'If you want to give me a really special gift,' the woman said to her husband, 'let me rule your kingdom for just one day.' The king told her that this was impossible, but she kept on at him with the same request, over and over, until the king, being a good man and loving his wife very much, said to her at last, 'For one day, because I love you so much my dear one, you may rule my kingdom.' She kissed him – making a great show of how much she appreciated the love he had shown her, and what does this woman do on her first day of ruling? With the help of the high executioner, she cuts off the head of her husband the king.

'But wait,' says the woman, beginning first in Greek and finding her lack of fluency a burden, protests now in English. 'What of all the kings who had their wives put to death? What of Henry, the English king?'

But they are not listening. They are bent on establishing the depravity of women. She sits back, comforting herself that she is witnessing male prejudice, as if in some experiment.

'I will tell you a better story,' says the man from Samos. He lights another cigarette, pausing for effect. His wife has come now from the change room and sits beside him. 'Kalimera,' she says to them and the Australian-born woman knows that she is Greek born and judges that she will give no support in pleading the cause of women. She sits arranging her hair with a hand mirror and a comb and completing her hair, begins to rub cream into her skin. The Australian-born woman turns away to focus again on the men waiting for the story to begin.

There was once a merchant who could not get on with his wife. She was a great trouble to him. Even though he bought her a house where she could live alone, she would still come to pester him. So he determined to do something about it.

A powerful wizard lived on the other side of the island. People said he was as old as the mountains and as crafty as a fox. The merchant decided to visit him.

'What do you want, my man?' asked the old wizard.

'I want you to get rid of a woman for me.'

'Ah, so you want me to kill your wife.'

'Sh – ' said the merchant, fearful that someone might hear.

'Well, what will you give me for that piece of work?'

'I will give you a bag of silver.'

'I have no use for silver.'

'Then I will give you a bag of gold.'

'I have no use for gold.'

'What on earth do you want me to give you?' said the merchant, desperate in case the wizard would not help him.

'You are a landholder?' asked the old magician. 'You grow olives?'

'Yes, I have terraces of olive trees.'

'And you press the olives into oil?'

'I make the finest oil on the island.'

'To get rid of your wife,' said the old wizard, 'you will need to bring me a year's supply of your best olive oil.'

'I will bring it. In a day's time, I will bring it.'

'You do not try to bargain, merchant. You must be a very wealthy man.'

'This woman has caused me much worry. I will be pleased to pay to be rid of her.'

'Listen to me, merchant. Listen and hear what I will do for you and for all the men on our island. Bring me five years' supply of oil, and I will not only remove your wife, I will get rid of all the women on the island.'

The men began to clap. It is a great story. A great story.

The Australian-born woman cannot believe her ears. She will have to recount this tale to her feminist friends at school.

The wife of the man from Samos has only now put her mirror and her jar of cream back into her toilet bag. She turns to her husband and says, 'Come Spiro. It is time we went to have lunch.'

'Ah yes, I had forgotten,' says the man from Samos. 'Do you know what we will eat today? Some smoked fish we bought from a compatriot in the town and some of our broad beans. We grew them in our garden. You have never seen such broad beans – big, but not dry . . .'

'Do not begin boasting about your garden Spiro,' his wife interrupts. 'It is time to go.'

'Be quiet, woman!' her husband shouts at her, and then he stands and raises his hand as if to strike her.

The Australian-born woman is furious. Do something, she signals to the other woman. Don't take this from him.

But the Greek woman does nothing and her husband, still holding up his hand, punctuates each word he says with a thrust of his fist towards her. 'Don't you forget. I have brought the olive oil.'

The men are laughing now – delighted by his wit as well as his demonstration of strength.

His wife continues silent, but as he stands, still threatening, she takes their two towels and hangs them on his upraised arm. She leans across and takes the rest of his belongings from the table and standing as tall as her husband, puts his cloth hat on his head and his packet of cigarettes and his lighter into his bathrobe pocket. 'Come now, Spiro,' she says smiling. 'Until you learn to look after yourself, you'd better keep your olive oil for your salad.'

The Larder

MORRIS LURIE 1984

'Larder of the earth, the sea. Man's richest feeding ground.'

The Great Barrier Reef, off the tropical coast of Queensland, delights tourists with its colourful coral, shells, fish and underwater plants. However, it is a sensitive ecological area which enthusiastic but careless visitors can affect by their presence.

Born in Melbourne, Morris Lurie is a Jewish writer of novels and short stories which have been widely published overseas.

'We Like White-man Alright', page 143, presents a very different relationship between humans and their natural environment.

The people who didn't go to the reef crowded around to see what the others had brought back. 'My goodness,' said one of the old ladies who hadn't gone (she had come for a rest, and was a little bit frightened of boats and water and all that stepping up and down), 'what are they?' She peered down at one of them, blinking. It lay on its back, on the grass, the creature tucked up inside its shell, only the tip of its claw visible, quite harmless, but the old lady wouldn't touch it. Some of the others were crawling about on the grass. The island dog sniffed at them and barked. 'Aren't they beautiful?' said the people who had brought them back, pushing them with their feet when they tried to creep away too far, out of the circle of light. Forty people had gone to the reef, and they had brought back almost a hundred shells. The tide was in, so the boat had been able to tie up at the quay, and they had stepped straight ashore, laughing, flushed with sun, exhausted, the usual tourists. When the tide was out, you were brought in by flat-bottomed barge, a slow and tiring business. The tide went out almost half a mile. It was night now, quite dark. The bells for dinner sounded through the trees. 'Is it safe to just leave them here?' the people who had brought them back wanted to know, because they were hungry and wanted to go in for dinner. 'Safe as houses,' said the guide. 'Turn them over, they won't get far.' So they turned them over and left them there on the grass, some of them wriggling, most of them still, with the island dog sniffing and growling and running around them in the night.

They talked about them over dinner, proudly. 'Oh, I brought back *nine*,' one of them said. He laughed. He was a real-estate agent with a huge face, loose jowls, shaggy eyebrows, his shirt open at the throat and his corduroy jacket loosely thrown over his shoulders, leaving his arms free while he ate. 'Don't know what the hell I'm going to do with them all, but there they were, free for the taking, you can't pass up a chance like that. Damn rare. Chance of a lifetime. God knows when I'll be in these parts again. Well, see that lady over there? – with the glasses? She brought back *twelve*. Love to see her getting all those home, ha ha. One of them about the size of this table.' 'Really?' said a lady who hadn't gone. She was a schoolteacher. 'That big?' 'Naah,' said the real-estate agent, laughing, his mouth full of food. 'I'm joking. But pretty big, all the same. About like this.' He showed her with his hands. She narrowed her eyes and shook her head. 'What *are* they exactly? What are they called?' she wanted to know. 'Don't ask me,' said the real-estate agent. 'Beautiful things, though. When you turn them over. Smooth as silk. You have to take the things out of them though, otherwise they really stink up the place.'

They had crawled quite far in the morning, some of them off the grass and onto the gravel paths, and a few of them even further and in amongst the trees, but they were all found and all brought back. The larger ones hadn't moved at all, their silk-smooth purple and mauve underside still pointed up to the sky. In some of them, the creature had come quite a way out, and you could see the pink of its body past the claw. But they all ducked back into their shells as soon as they were touched, except for the very tip of the claw, for which there was no room in the shell. They were lightning fast. They had already started to smell. A few of them looked dead.

The owners of the shells gathered around them, poking them with their feet, picking them up, turning them over, comparing shells, boasting of their own. But a few of them, seeing them now in the sun, appeared slightly embarrassed. They had brought back so many! Yesterday's enthusiasm hung on a thread. In the bright morning sun, under the palms, you could see how ugly they were, spiky, as rough as rocks, crawling slowly on the grass. But their undersides, in the morning sun, were more beautiful than ever.

A few of them set straight to work to get the creatures out. The others watched, not knowing what to do. It was hard to get hold of the claw, and even when you did, it was impossible to pull the creature out. It hung on grimly, locked inside its shell. You could pull them out about an inch, no more. And once you let go, the creature would hastily withdraw, and that was that. It wouldn't venture out again, unless you left it alone for over an hour.

'Bastards, aren't they?' said the real-estate agent. He had sat himself down on the grass and had one in his lap and was scratching away at the creature with a long-bladed knife, trying to gouge it out. 'That's awfully cruel,' said the schoolteacher, and shuddered. The real-estate agent laughed. 'Naah,' he said. 'They don't feel a thing. Larder of the earth, the sea. Man's richest feeding ground. There's plenty more where this came from, and getting this fella out won't make any difference at all. Pity they're not edible though.' He continued gouging with his knife, squinting in the sun, enjoying his work.

It was impossible to get them out with knives and sticks. Someone tried a fishhook but that tore through the creature, which quickly withdrew, leaving a wet colourless smear on the shell. Wire was useless. Throwing them about on the grass didn't do anything at all. Putting them in water to coax the creatures out and then using a knife was a waste of time. It was half-way through the morning and no one had succeeded in removing a single one.

But they kept at it, undaunted. They sat about on the grass, under the trees, smoking cigarettes and trying everything they could think of and calling out suggestions to each other. 'Why not just leave them in the sun?' someone suggested. 'Let the ants eat them out.' 'They'll smell for months,' was the reply to that.

Then someone hit upon an idea. Everyone gathered around him and he explained it. 'Fishing line,' he said. 'Make a noose around the claw and then hang the shell up and the weight of it will drag the things out.' He showed them how. In thirty minutes they had hung them all up. They hung them from shrubs and from low branches and from railings. Everywhere you looked there were shells hanging. The method began to work at once. You could see the shells inching down to the ground, the creatures stretching, more and more of them coming out, pink in the sun. In ten minutes, some of them had pulled out as much as six inches, thin and pink, with the shell swaying under them. The owners of the shells watched, fascinated, until the bells rang for lunch, and then they went off to wash their hands and to eat.

All through lunch you could hear the shells dropping, plop, plop, softly on to the grass, regularly, one after another. You could see them lying on the ground through the windows of the dining room, like coconuts, except for the spikes. And you could also see those that hadn't yet dropped, hanging low, the creatures stretched to a foot and more, the shells swaying and rocking under them though there was no wind.

The people who had hung them up were very happy at lunch. 'There goes another!' they called out, each time one fell to the ground. There was a lot of laughing and joking. They made bets to see which ones would drop first. The fishing line idea, they agreed, had been a stroke of genius.

By the time the main course arrived, they had all dropped. The grass was littered with shells. Those that had fallen with their undersides up shone in the sun. Most of them fell the other way, rough side up, the way they had looked on the reef, where you could hardly tell them from rock, except for the movement.

Then the birds came. They came just as the dessert was being served. They wheeled in the sky, scores of them, their wings flapping, screaming, crying, swooping down with their beaks open, flashes of white and grey, with red legs and orange beaks. They came for the things on the fishing lines, hanging from the trees. You could smell the things through the open windows of the dining room, as rank as the sea, salty and foul. The attack of the birds was sudden and swift. It was all over before coffee.

After lunch, the people who had brought the shells back from the reef collected their shells and stacked them up outside their rooms, ready to take home with them. It was wonderful, they said, how cleanly the creatures had come out. The shells were not harmed at all.

They left the next morning, early, while the tide was still in. They took about twenty shells with them. They took only the smallest ones, those about the size of your hand. They were a good size, they said, for your mantelpiece. The others were ludicrous. They laughed, imagining them in their homes. Anyhow, they couldn't possibly fit them all into their luggage. The shells they didn't want they left outside their rooms. After the tourists had gone, the unwanted shells were pushed into a pile and thrown away, like the unwanted shells of the week before, and the week before that, and the week before that.

In the afternoon, a fresh boatful of tourists came in. They had come to swim and to drink and to laze in the sun. But already they were eager for their trip to the reef. They had been promised a treat. Their trip to the reef would take place on the day of the lowest tide of the year.

Warrigal

DAL STIVENS 1968

'Like ourselves animals are land owners.'

For many Australian families, their ideal is to live in a house surrounded by lawns and a garden, in the suburbs of a town or city. What happens when a 'suburbanite' brings home a dingo, a wolf-like native dog that roams the outback? Dingoes were domesticated by Aboriginal people, who called them 'warrigal'.

Dal Stivens was important as a writer of short stories from the 1930s onwards.

White Australians have often credited the dingo with great intelligence as a predator, as in 'The Three-legged Bitch', page 125.

'You'll have to get rid of that dingo before long,' my neighbour Swinburne said to me across the fence. 'Why, he's an Asiatic wolf – '

'No one of any authority says that the dingo is an Asiatic wolf,' I said. 'The Curator of Mammals at the Australian Museum classifies the dingo as *Canis familiaris* variety *dingo* – that is, a variety of the common dog. Another eminent authority says it's most unlikely that the dingo is descended from the northern wolf – '

'I know a wolf when I see it,' this classic pyknic said. 'I don't care what some long-haired professors say. I was brought up in the bush.'

As my wife Martha says, I can be insufferable at times – particularly when I'm provoked. I said: 'So much for your fears of this animal attacking you – it's most unlikely as long as he continues to look on you as the *gamma* animal. Of course, you need to act like a *gamma* animal at all times.'

I thought for a moment he was going to climb over the paling fence that divided our properties and throw a punch at me.

'You be careful who you call an animal!' he said. His big red face and neck were swelling like a frog's. It was pure Lorenz and Heidigger I was throwing at him. This was during my animal behaviour period.

'I'm not calling you an animal,' I said. 'I'm just explaining how the dingo sees you. He sees me as the *alpha* animal – *alpha* is Greek for A. I'm the pack leader in his eyes. He sees my wife, Martha, as the *beta* animal. *Beta* is B and

In the Shadow of the Wall by Ron Hawke, acrylic on canvas.

gamma is C. He probably sees you and your wife and kids as *gamma* or *delta* animals. *Delta* is D. While you behave like *gamma* or *delta* animals, you'll be O.K. He'll defer to you.'

He seemed a little assured – or confused, anyway.

'This *gamma* stuff,' he began uncertainly. 'You're sure of it, now?'

'I'll lend you a book,' I said.

'All the same, he's got pretty powerful jaws,' he said, pointing to Red, who was crouching at my feet, his eyes not leaving me. The jaws were, as he said, powerful, and the white shining canine teeth rather large. The head was a little too large, the prick ears a bit too thick at the roots for Red to be a really handsome dog, but there was a compact power in his strong tawny chest and limbs.

'No more than a German shepherd's,' I said. There were two of them in Mansion Road – that wasn't the name but it will do.

'I suppose so,' he said doubtfully.

'If I hadn't told you Red was a dingo you wouldn't be worrying,' I said. 'I could have told you Red was a mongrel.'

'Are you trying to tell me I wouldn't know a dingo?' he started in belligerently.

Before I could answer, his own dog, a Dobermann Pinscher and a real North Shore status job, came out and began challenging Red. Both dogs raced up and down on their sides of the fence, the Pinscher growling and barking and Red just growling. (Dingoes don't bark in the wilds. When domesticated some learn to do so but Red hadn't.)

Red ran on his toes, his reddish-brown coat gleaming and white-tipped bushy tail waving erect. His gait was exciting to watch: it was smooth, effortless and one he could maintain for hours.

'This is what I mean,' he said. 'Your Asiatic wolf could savage my dog to death.'

'Yours is making the most noise,' I said. The Pinscher was as aggressive as his master.

'Noise isn't everything,' he said. 'Look at that wolf-like crouching.'

'Innate behaviour,' I said. 'Dingoes have acquired that over thousands of years of attacking emus and kangaroos. They crouch to avoid the kicks.'

'So your wolf is getting ready to attack, is he?'

'Not necessarily,' I said. 'No more than yours is. Of course, if one dog were to invade the other's territory, then there would be a fight. But they won't invade.'

'Yours could jump the fence,' he said. 'I've seen him. He could kill my dog and clean up my fowls.'

'Not into your place,' I said. I was beginning to lose my temper. 'He wouldn't. He knows it isn't his.'

'So he's moral, is he?' he shouted. 'This wild dog – '

'They're all moral although the term is anthropomorphic. Wild dogs or domestic dogs usually won't invade another's territory.'

'So you say,' he said. His face was purpling. 'I warn you now yours had better not. If he does I'll shoot him. The law's on my side.'

I was so angry I went inside and got a hammer. I started knocking palings out of the fence.

'Hey!' he shouted. 'That's my fence. And I meant what I said about shooting that Asiatic mongrel.'

'Pure-bred dingo,' I grunted. I was out of condition and the nails were tough. 'Our fence.'

I got four palings out and, as I knew would happen, the dogs kept racing past the gap and ignoring the chance to enter and attack. I was dishing out pure Lorenz.

'It's just bluff,' I said. 'You can see it for yourself. They talk big. After they've said their bit, they'll knock off.'

'Perhaps,' he said, doubtfully.

'Call your dog out into the street,' I said. 'I'll call mine. They'll meet in the middle and sniff each other's anal quarters but they won't fight. There's nothing to fight about – none lays claim to the centre of the road. Of course, the footpath is different.'

'I won't risk it,' he said and he called the Pinscher and started off. 'You may be right and your dingo ought to be at home in your garden.'

It might have sounded conciliatory to you. But there was a crack in it. This was during my Australian native flora period. When I bought this block I had the house built well down the hillside and left all the trees and shrubs. I wanted a native bushland garden and I had left what the other people in Mansion Road called 'that rubbish' in its near-natural state. I had planted some more natives – waratahs like great red Roman torches, delicately starred wax flowers and native roses, piquantly scented boronias, flannel flowers, and subtly curving spider flowers. This was in keeping with my newly acquired feeling for *furyu*, which is often used to describe things Japanese. It can be translated as 'tasteful', but the Japanese characters convey a fuller meaning of 'flowing with the wind' – the acceptance of nature, of the material itself, and of the patterns it imposes. Transferring the concept to Australia, I was accepting nature and learning to appreciate the muted beauty of Australian shrubs and flowers.

The neighbours didn't approve. They all had lots of lawns and terraces and beds of perennials and annuals. They'd chopped down most of the native trees and planted exotics. They thought my garden lowered the tone of the street. And they thought the same about our unobtrusive low-line house, blending with the slim eucalypts and the sandstone outcrops. They preferred double-fronted mod. bungs.

We'd have got on a lot better if we had lived in Mansion Street during my azalea and camellia period. At our last house Martha and I had gone in for landscaping – vistas, focus points, and the rest. And we'd used azaleas and camellias for much of the mass planting. I'd got myself wised up on azaleas, particularly, and I knew as much as most about Wilson's fifty Kurumes; I once engaged in some learned discussion in a specialist journal as to whether or not some experts were correct in thinking Pink Pearl (*Azuma kagami*) was, indeed, the progenitor of all the pink-flowered forms.

That was some time ago, and although I still like azaleas, the love affair was then over. Not everyone appreciates Australian natives. We went away for a week once and when we came back someone had dumped two tons of rubbish into our place. We had no fence at the street level and someone had thought it was a virgin block. The house is well down the slope and hard to see from the street. Of course, he should have noticed the rather heavy concentration of native flora. He had tipped the rusting tins, galvanised iron, mattresses, and so on, onto a stand of native roses, too.

We didn't really fit into Mansion Road for a number of reasons. First, there was my profession as a journalist and writer. And moreover, Martha and I were in our Chagall period; our earlier Rembrandt love affair might have been accepted.

And there was the car business. They all had one or two cars but we didn't see the need when there was a good taxi and hire car service. When they finally got the idea that we could afford a car but wouldn't have one, it struck them as un-Australian or something.

The dingo business was merely another straw, though Swinburne seemed to be trying to push it a bit further.

'Why get yourself angry?' Martha reproached me when I went inside.

'A conformist ass!' I said.

'You can't educate him,' she said.

'I know,' I said. 'I was having a bit of fun.'

'Whatever you call it, we'll probably have to get rid of Red,' she said.

'Where?' I said.

That was the question. I wasn't giving him to the Zoo, as some in Mansion Road had hinted I should. Dingoes are far-ranging, lively, intelligent creatures and it would be cruelty to confine him. And I couldn't release him in the bush now that he was a year old and had had no training in hunting for himself. Normally, he would have acquired this from his mother, but I'd got Red as a pup. A zoologist friend had brought him to Sydney and then found his wife wouldn't let him keep a dingo.

I didn't see Swinburne again until the next weekend. He called me over the fence.

'What you say about that dingo might be true at present but he'll revert to type,' he said. 'The hunting instinct is too strong. It will be someone's chicken run eventually even if it's not mine.'

'He hasn't been taught to hunt fowls – or anything else,' I said. 'So why should he? He's well fed.'

'Primitive instincts are strong,' said Swinburne.

'We don't know what his primeval instincts are,' I said.

'He's a wild dog.'

I said, insufferably: 'Professor Konrad Lorenz, who is one of the world's greatest authorities on dogs, says that the dingo is a descendant of a domesticated dog brought here by the Aborigines. He points out that a pure-blooded dingo often has white stockings or stars and nearly always a white tip to its tail. He adds that these points are quite irregularly distributed. This, as everyone knows, is a feature never seen in wild animals but it occurs frequently in all domestic animals.'

'Has this foreign professor ever seen a dingo in the wilds?' he asked.

I couldn't see what his question had to do with the paraphrase I had given him, but I told him that while Lorenz had not been to Australia so far as I knew, he had bred and studied dingoes.

He changed the subject abruptly.

'You seem to know all about animals and birds,' he said. 'Perhaps you have a cure for a crowing rooster? Mine is upsetting some of the neighbours by crowing during the night. He answers other roosters across the valley.'

(There were farms there.) 'In a street like Mansion Road, you have to fit in.'
He was getting at me but I ignored it.

'I think so,' I said.

'I'd like to hear it,' he said, too sweetly.

'You have to get on with people, as you say,' I said, also too sweetly. 'But roosters can be stopped from crowing in a very simple fashion. A rooster, as you know, has to stretch its neck to crow. I'd suggest tacking a piece of hessian over the perch, a couple of inches above his head. When he goes to stretch his neck, he'll bump the hessian and won't be able to crow.'

He took it in after a few questions and said he'd try it. It took him and his fifteen-year-old son most of the afternoon. I must say they were thorough. It took them ten minutes to catch that White Leghorn and then they held him with his feet on the ground and measured the distance to a couple of inches over his head. They measured the hessian meticulously and then they had a conference during which they kept looking towards me. I was sowing some flannel flower seeds. I'd gone to the nearby bushland reserve several times to observe the soil and aspect of flannel flowers so that I could plant the seeds in the right place in my garden.

Swinburne came over to the fence finally. 'I'm sorry to trouble you,' he said. This was a change. 'But there are several perches in the hen house.'

'The top one,' I said. 'He's the *alpha* animal.'

They fixed it there and Swinburne asked me to come and have a beer at his place. But he hadn't changed his mind much about the dingo because he and his wife started telling me about the merits of budgerigars as pets.

'Now, budgerigars make marvellous pets,' he said. 'Our Joey is a wonderful talker.'

The bird, a male pied blue, was perched on his hand, and while Mrs Swinburne smiled dotingly, it displayed and then, with wings down-dragging, it tried to copulate with Swinburne's big red hand.

'Isn't he quaint?' asked Mrs Swinburne. 'He does that by the hour.'

Poor bloody bird, I thought.

'No wonder,' I said aloud.

'What do you mean?'

'Nothing,' I said. 'I mean it's wonderful.'

'And they tell me budgerigars don't talk in the wilds,' said Mrs Swinburne.

'No,' I said. 'Only when they're caged.' I refrained from saying anything about mimicry being due to starved sexuality, to banked-up energy.

I couldn't see Mansion Road letting up on Red – Swinburne was just the official spokesman as it were, one of the *alpha* members in the street, the managing director of a shoe factory. I knew the others were saying the same things among themselves.

They said them to me a few nights later. Mrs Fitter called. If Swinburne was an *alpha* male, she was *the alpha* female. Her father had been a drapery knight and had built the big house in which the Fitters lived with a feature window and two cars.

'I've come on behalf of the mothers of Mansion Road,' she started in. She was a large dark woman with a hint of a moustache. 'They're very frightened that ravening wild dingo will attack their children. They have to pass it on their way to school and it crouches in the gutter.'

She was laying it on. Most of the children were driven to school.

'It won't attack them,' I said. 'He lies in the gutter because that's his territorial boundary. Like ourselves animals are land owners.'

'And what's more he barks at them,' she said, going too far.

'Dingoes don't bark,' I said, gently, but I was getting angry. Martha was making signs.

'And at cars, too,' she said. 'I had to swerve to miss him. And he slavers at the lips.'

'He has well-developed salivary glands,' I said. 'I assure you he won't attack anyone, but in any case the solution is simple. Your Schnauzer owns your footpath, Mrs Fitter – or thinks he does. I respect his property right and don't walk on his footpath and we get on very well.'

It wasn't tactful but I didn't want to be.

After Mrs Fitter had left, Martha said, 'Red has been going out after cars the last couple of days.'

'But not barking?' I asked.

'No,' she said.

Three nights later a young policeman called. Mrs Fitter had complained that Red had killed one of her fowls.

'Did she see him?' I asked.

'No, but she is convinced it could only have been the dingo,' he said.

'Well, constable, you know the legal position as well as I do,' I said. I didn't like it but I had to tack a bit. 'Every dog is allowed one bite – but not two. I don't admit that Red did kill the fowl. It could have been any one of the dogs in the street. And, further, Red is not necessarily a dingo. He could be a mongrel. I don't know his parentage. He was found in the outback by a friend and brought to Sydney.'

He went away but was back the next night.

'Mrs Fitter says that you have admitted that the animal is a dingo,' he said.

'I admit nothing,' I said tacking again. 'I have called the dog a dingo without any accurate knowledge and purely out of a spirit of fantasy. I wanted to indulge in a little fancy. It has been fun to think of Red as a dingo.'

He was a bit shaken and I went on, 'I'm no expert on dingoes, nor is anyone else in this street. Have you ever seen a pure-bred dingo?'

'I think so – at the Zoo – ' he said, uncertainly.

'Exactly,' I said. 'And how do you know it was a pure one and even if it was, would you be able to point to any dog with certainty and say that is a dingo or that another was a Dobermann Pinscher – '

'A Dobermann what, sir?'

'Mr Swinburne's dog is a Dobermann Pinscher. Mrs Fitter, on the other hand, has a Schnauzer. Of course, the two have points in common, according to the experts. I am told that a Manchester Terrier is even closer in appearance to a Dobermann Pinscher and that only the well informed can pick one from the other. Now when you come to mongrels, the question of identification is much more complicated – '

There was a bit more of it. He fled in some confusion and Martha and I rolled around the floor, helpless with laughter, and went to bed earlier. But it was getting serious. If I didn't cure Red of going out on the road, Mrs Fitter, or someone else, wasn't going to swerve next time.

What I did was undiluted Lorenz.

If you want to stop a dog chasing cars you have to fire a small stone at him from behind from a catapult when he is in the middle of chasing. When you do it this way the dog is taken by surprise. He doesn't see you do it and it seems to him like the hand of God. That is anthropomorphic, but you know what I'm getting at; it's a memorable experience for the dog and usually cures him completely.

I stayed home the next day. It took me an hour to make a catapult that worked properly and I had to practise for twenty minutes. Then I was ready. I cured Red that morning with two hits, which were, I hope, not too painful. The gutter and the street were abandoned by him. Encouraged, I decided to cure him of establishing himself on the footpath. I achieved that, too.

I knew it only won a respite for the dingo. I had to return him to the wilds.

The alternatives of giving him to the Zoo, or having him put away, I'd already rejected. Swinburne came home early that day.

'I see you're still insisting on keeping that Asiatic wolf,' he said.

'*Canis familiaris* variety *dingo*,' I corrected. 'But you're wrong about keeping him. I'm returning him to the wilds.'

'But they're sheep killers.'

'Not where there are no sheep.'

'There are sheep everywhere,' he said stubbornly.

'Australia's a big place,' I said. 'There ought to be a place somewhere where he can live his own life. But he'll have to be taught to hunt before I can release him.'

'You mean on wild animals?'

'What else?' I said.

'You'll soon have the fauna protection people after you,' he said.

'Rabbits aren't protected,' I said.

'They're vermin – and so are dingoes!' he said.

They didn't give me time to put my plan into operation. I had thought it just possible that they might give Red a bait. But I couldn't believe they hated him so much. Besides it's an offence to lay baits and they were most law-abiding in Mansion Road. They didn't poison Red. What happened was that Red went wandering off one day through the bushland reserve and a poultry farmer on the other side of the valley shot the dingo, as he was legally entitled to do.

'Sorry to hear about that dog of yours,' said Swinburne later.

'But why should he go off?' I asked.

'I know a bit about dingoes,' he said and his eyes were gleaming. 'Most likely he followed a bitch on heat. It's a question of studying animal behaviour.'

I knew then that he'd done it with a farmer in on the job. They were legal in Mansion Road. But I wouldn't be able to prove anything.

'It's better to keep budgerigars as pets,' I said, blazing inside. 'You keep them sex-starved and they'll try to mate with your hand.' Only I used a blunter word. 'It's all nice and jolly and they'll talk, too.'

I was sorry afterwards for losing my temper. Swinburne wrung the budgerigar's neck the next time it displayed on his wife's hand.

We sold out soon afterwards. I was coming to the end of my Australian native flora period, anyway.

Day Trip to Surfers b/w Get Lost Adorno

CRAIG McGREGOR 1985

'A bit further on there was what Mum called a classic Australian scene: a range of hills in the distance, shining blue bitumen, a bit of old truck tyre, and a dead wallaby on the side of the road. "One of Australia's fur-lined highways," said Jack Jr.'

This could be just a comic tale of a family's 'day trip' by car from Sydney to Surfers Paradise on the coast of Queensland – a distance of about 900 kilometres – and the jokey, slangy talk with which they pass the time. (Many Australian travellers take such long distances in their stride.) The ending, however, suggests that the story can be read in a number of different ways.

Craig McGregor is a university teacher in Sydney.

In 'Going Home', page 53, Billy Woodward's journey brings him to a very different kind of destination.

We decided to leave early so we could make it in one day. Dad said it would save the cost of a motel. Mum said it would give us an extra day's holiday. Jack Junior said he wanted to spend a week in the heart of the beast. Minnie, who's the young one, and me just went along.

The alarm went off at 3.30 a.m. After two hours of arguing and packing we were ready to leave. We got as far as Oxford Street when Mum decided she'd left the stove on when she'd boiled the eggs. We drove back, very sceptical. She had. The saucepan was still boiling. 'Could've burnt the bloody place down,' said Dad. 'Would've been better if it had,' said Jack Jr, who is very into pessimism. He is trying to form a rock band with me as lead singer. I am writing a Lou Reed type number for him called *You're So Negative*.

About Hornsby it started to get light. We got as far as the s-bends leading onto the Newcastle Expressway before Brian the Dog threw up. All over the back of the station wagon. He gets carsick easily. We'd starved him for a day but he still threw up. Maybe that's why. Minnie came to his defence. 'Look at his tail, he looks like a little teapot you could pour out,' she said. Everyone fell asleep.

First stop was the Oak milk bar near the Pacific Highway turnoff. It was packed with daytrippers eating scallops and chips. Brian kept barking at a small pale dog with a cur-like tail in the campervan parked three cars down. Mum came back with some cups of coffee and noticed the dog. 'Whippet! Whip it good!' she said.

After that everyone cheered up. The car reeked of Pine-O-Kleen instead of dog spew. Dad heard some cicadas in the bush just past Raymond Terrace and began singing, in mock-Spanish, 'CI-CA-DA!' He reckons I get my voice from him but I hope not. Jack Jr put on a Divinyls tape to drown him out. Dad insisted on singing along with it; he likes the part where Chrissie Amphlett flaps her lips like a dumb punk. 'Next time I'll bring along a Charlie Parker tape,' said Jack Jr. 'See if you can sing to that.'

Myall Lakes. 'Myall is what Aborigines call white people,' said Mum. 'It means ghosts.' Jack Jr said: 'They're the ghosts.'

Minnie found some cobwebs in the rear window slot. Then she found a spider. Our last car, a rustbucket Holden, was infested with cockroaches. We're like a travelling Mr Flick ad. Our family is very ecology conscious. When we passed a truckload of pink Berkshire pigs Mum was concerned. 'I hope they're not sunburnt,' she said. Then we passed some swans swimming in that artificial lake outside the power station north of Newcastle. 'Those swans are too low in the water,' Mum said. 'They look as though they've got weights on their legs,' Mum said. 'Oh my god,' Dad said.

Between Coolongolook and Rainbow Flat, which is a goodly distance, Minnie insisted on recounting, scene by scene, the entire story of *The Life of Brian*. Brian the Film can only stand so much retelling. Brian the Dog snored on.

The day was hotting up. Dad was still driving, Mum was in the passenger seat looking at a map, Jack Jr and me and Minnie were in the back seat, and Brian was lying across the luggage in the station wagon section. He woke up when Dad swore at a semitrailer and kept trying to infiltrate the back seat. He stunk. There was a lot of traffic on the road and we had to keep passing caravans at speed. We had so much gear on the roofrack that the roof started flapping up and down like a tent. 'If they made that sheet metal any thinner you could roll your own with it,' Dad said. Once we passed a lowloader with one of those huge three-storey ocean-going marlin launches on it. 'Doctor,' said Dad. 'Lawyer,' said Mum. 'Political chief,' said Jack Jr. A bit further on

Barbara Hanrahan (1939–91) was a writer as well as an artist, who drew on her memories of growing up with her mother and mother's family. As their clothing shows, the people in this print are figures from her childhood in the 1940s and 1950s – a generation before the family in 'Day Trip to Surfers'.

My Family – My Australia by Barbara Hanrahan, 1982, in *Barbara Hanrahan: Printmaker* by Alison Carroll.

there was a Rest Area which Mum called a Lay-By. 'Can you help me pay it off?' I whined. It was my first joke of the trip.

At Taree we stopped for petrol and to give Brian a chance to have a piss. He refused. Sometimes Dad has to piss into the bush beside him to give Brian the idea but the petrol station was a bit public. Dad slammed the tailgate down and we set off again. Brian seemed strangely immobile; he'd stopped slithering over the luggage towards the front seat. It was about five minutes before Minnie realised his tail was caught in the tailgate. 'At least it stopped him trying to drive,' said Dad.

Jack Jr is trying to work out a name for his band. We spent about fifty kilometres helping. 'Call it something sexy like The Aphro-disiacs,' said Dad. 'Deck yourself out in big bushy black hairdos.' I suggested a sort of Latin/Oz fusion: Carlos Lantana and the Weedkillers. Mum said G-Spot was a good name but she didn't know what it meant. Dad said he didn't either. Mum said what he meant was he didn't know where it was. Jack Jr said a sparring partner was a blonde in a Jacuzzi. We passed a sign saying KOALAS PASS HERE. Dad reckoned he could see the bear droppings. Minnie reckoned Bear Drops was a good name for a nudist cold cure. I had a sudden flash: 'Why don't you call the band Drop Bears?' 'Don't be stupid,' said Jack Jr, 'who would ever listen to a group called Drop Bears?'

Near Coppernook there was a big stand of gnarled angophoras. 'Nature abhors a straight line,' said Dad, who is collecting aphorisms. His own. A bit further on there was what Mum called a classic Australian scene: a range of hills in the distance, shining blue bitumen, a bit of old truck tyre, and a dead wallaby on the side of the road. 'One of Australia's fur-lined highways,' said Jack Jr. Minnie said: 'The kids at our school call the Vietnamese kids slopes.' 'Racism,' said Dad. I said: 'Do you know how many Californians it takes to change a lightbulb? Eighteen. One to change the bulb and seventeen to share the experience.' 'More racism,' said Dad. 'Better than tokenism,' I said, practising my feminism. 'There's nothing wrong with tokenism as long as you're at the top of the tokenpole,' Dad said. Jack Jr started making pig noises. Mum joined in. Dad drove on.

We were well into the Central Coast and cruising through a little place south of Wauchope when we noticed a policeman standing on the side of the road. Incongruous. He had a noticeboard in his hand. It said PULL OVER. Radar trap. Dad was breathalysed and then booked for doing 79 kph in a 60 kph zone. 'They're practising for 1984,' said Jack Jr. 'This is 1984,' I said. 'That's what I mean,' said Jack Jr.

Dad got back into the car grumbling about the cops picking on him because of the surfboards on the roofrack. 'Didn't realise I was a family man on holidays,' he said. Just north of Port Macquarie the police-magnet problem was solved abruptly when the boards flew off the top of the car. They went bouncing down the bitumen and the car behind had to swerve to miss them. As the driver went past he shouted out something indecipherable. It was probably a compliment. We went back and rescued the boards. Dad's Malibu was all right but Minnie's foamie had a big hole chopped out of it. She started to cry.

'It's all right darling,' Mum said, 'we'll get the dings fixed in Surfers Paradise.'

'You can't fix dings in foamies,' Minnie sobbed.

'Heaps bad luck,' I said.

This time Dad roped the boards to the roofrack instead of using octopus straps. I climbed into the back seat and put my arm around Minnie. 'It's all right for you,' she said. 'You're not learning re-entries.' I put my mouth up against her ear, the one with the coral earring – when she's not a surfie she's practising to be a droog – and whispered: 'Dad's a turkey!' She almost smiled.

At Telegraph Point Mum said she could do with a cup of tea.

At Kundabung I said I'd like one too.

At South Kempsey a semitrailer with a sign on top saying THE RESURRECTION nearly wiped us off the road.

At Poisonous Passionfruit Creek Dad tried to overtake a caravan without giving himself enough room, ran into double yellow lines, and pulled back just before a Nissan Turbo charged into us head-on.

'I think it's time we stopped, Jack,' Mum said.

At the next place, which didn't seem to have a name, we had a cup of tea. 'Unreal,' I said when I saw the Space Invaders machine. Mum said she thought the bloke behind the counter was gay. She once said flying Qantas was like Oxford Street in the air. She's a hetero. I assume Dad is. I'm bi by style, separatist by philosophy, but conformist by inclination. Mum says I'm multifaceted. Dad says I'm all over the place like a dog's breakfast.

I prefer Mum to Dad.

Mum took over the driving. She's good but slow. Approaching Nambucca

Heads we got caught behind a truck for kilometre after kilometre. The cicadas sounded like the roar of a reef break. 'Have I got a godmother?' Minnie asked. The cicadas roared. The roofrack hummed. It was getting near midday. We had travelled maybe five hundred kilometres since dawn. The truck was still up ahead. 'Sounds like the cicadas we used to have on the farm near Mullumbimby,' said Dad. 'They love she-oaks. I remember the first time Grandpa and Grandma and the family moved there. The cicadas started up down by the creek, just about sunset, and I'd never heard them so loud. And then this other noise started up, a deep sort of rumble which seemed to echo all around the hills. I thought it must have been a neighbour's petrol pump or milkin' machine.' He paused. 'Tree frogs. At least that's what they reckoned. Seemed to be up every tree, bloody deafening. It was years before I realised they were havin' me on. Different sort of cicada, starts up when the others leave off. Little black buggers. Black Princes we used to call 'em. Others were Greengrocers . . .'

He stopped. Everyone was asleep except me, and I was pretending. The story dribbled to a halt.

Dad's got dark splotches on his arm, just like Aunt Freda did when she died. He's going to die, too, one of these days. Edna Everage reckons you can tell the widows on tourist buses because they've all got their hubbies' wristwatches on their arms. Me, I like freckles; I've got 'em. But I don't like old-age splotches.

About Sawtell we decided to help Jack Jr name his rock band again.

'What about Funky Nipper?' said Minnie.

'Lead singer, Nip Jagger,' I said.

'It's a political group, we want a political name,' said Jack Jr crossly.

'What about Gramsci, The Group?' Mum said.

'What about Che?' I said.

'What about Che Sera Sera?' said Minnie.

'The next punster gets punished,' said Dad.

'Forget it,' said Jack Jr.

We stopped for lunch at Coffs Harbour, at the Big Banana. Mum said the Whitlam government had been going to turn it into a major city; they were going to rename it Gough's Harbour. The Big Banana is the biggest asbestos cement banana in the world; you can walk through it. Minnie crawled through it backwards. The souvenir shop was full of stuff from Taiwan. The milk bar sold chocolate-coated bananas. We ate rolls and had a banana-flavoured Dairy Freeze each in the open-air cafeteria. Tourists in funny hats were pouring in one end and walking out with trays at the other. For fast food it was pretty slow. The loudspeakers were tuned to the local radio station; they pumped out UB40, David Bowie, the Angels, Mentals, Bow Wow Wow, Spandau Ballet, Wham, Sharon O'Neill, Grand Master Flash, Goanna, Haysi Fantasi, Culture Club and Dylan. In between the ads. There was no band called Lantana. Bobby sang:

Capitalism is above the law
They say it don't count unless it sells . . .

Jack Jr looked up from his Chiko roll. 'It's never gunna change,' he said, 'until it's all torn down.'

Mum said: 'That's all very well, Jack, but in the meantime we have to resist it . . .'

Jack Jr said: 'You can't resist it. Adorno says it pervades everything, we're all manipulated and given artificial appetites and turned into consumers . . .'

Minnie said: 'I'm still hungry.'

Dad said: 'Have another Chiko roll.'

I said: 'Who's Adorno?'

Mum said: 'If we wait until it's all torn down we'll be in our graves; what do we do in the meantime?'

Jack Jr said: 'He's a Marxist.'

Mum said: 'A somewhat omniscient one.'

I said: 'You mean he's a control freak?'

Bobby sang:

Democracy don't rule the world
You better get that through your head
This world is ruled by violence
But I guess that's better left unsaid . . .

'Look at this!' said Jack Jr, gesturing around at the Big Banana. 'This is our culture! Created and sold to us proles because we don't know any better. Pop culture is a control device. It makes you sick.'

'I like it,' I said.

'I sometimes think,' said Jack Jr, who was warming up, 'that Vitamin C is the perfect capitalist product. You can only absorb so much, your body disposes of the rest. Then next day you have to absorb some more.'

'I reckon your mother's right,' said Dad.

'I'm going to the Men's,' said Jack Jr.

'You went at the last Shell station,' said Mum, who is a schoolteacher and keeps track of these things.

'I'm going,' Jack Jr said, swaggering to his feet, '*because it's there.*'

We all trooped out in the glaring sunshine to the carpark. Brian was asleep on top of the Christmas presents. At least we didn't have a double-tailgate. As we pulled out onto the Pacific Highway two police cars came powering down the hill like American stock car racers. The front one had its siren going. We joined the line of traffic heading north.

'I don't care what it is,' said Dad, who had taken over the driving again, 'as long as it's not an accident.'

A few minutes later there was another siren. A big Ford F100 ambulance came up behind and then disappeared up ahead. No-one said anything. The traffic had slowed down perceptibly.

About ten kilometres ahead we came across the accident. We could tell because the cars heading south had their headlights on; a couple flashed them. There were two cars on the opposite sides of the highway, badly damaged. One was upside down. There was a crowd of people talking to the police, arguing.

There was no-one lying on the road shoulder, no-one kneeling down.

'Thank God for that,' Dad said, and overtook the car ahead.

Brian farted. Jack Jr blamed me. Everyone opened the windows.

'I'd like a big dog when I grow up,' Minnie said worriedly, 'but I don't know what sort. Red setters are dumb. Alsatians are too fierce. Dobermans get fat. Sheep dogs are a worry. Greyhounds are ridiculous. Terriers are too yappy. Cocker spaniels get ticks. Great Danes cost too much. Boxers are vicious. Whippets are cowardly . . .'

'WHIP IT! WHIP IT GOOD!' everyone shouted, and fell about the car. It had become a family serial joke.

We passed Woolgoolga at 110 kph.

'Living in Woolgoolga', said Jack Jr, 'must be about as interesting as watching a plank warp.'

Later afternoon. Mum was driving again. Dad had his head propped against a pillow on the passenger side window. The bitumen had that harsh afternoon glare to it. Driving through a State Forest the tree trunk shadows flashed on and off like a disco strobe.

Everyone was getting tired. We started arguing. I said I might become a hippie instead of a rock star. Mum said a resistant culture was more important than a counter-culture. Jack Jr wanted a go at driving. Dad said he wasn't experienced enough to handle holiday traffic. Mum said he'd never get experience if he didn't drive. We pulled up at a Golden Fleece service station. Jack Jr said if he wasn't allowed to drive then he wasn't going to bloody well wash the windscreen either. Minnie got a milkshake. Brian got another chance for a piss. Dad got a packet of Fantales. The first wrapper had a thing about Boy George on it. 'Fantales aren't what they used to be,' Dad said. 'If I wanted to read this shit I'd have asked for a packet of Androgynes.'

Nobody laughed. We had been on the road for twelve hours.

At the Byron Bay turnoff we all wanted to go for a surf – we being the kids. 'The boards are buggered,' said Dad. 'A swim then.' 'We'll never get to Surfers,' said Mum. By the time we'd finished discussing it we'd reached Tyagarah. The highway stretched ahead. We'd passed the turnoff. 'How do you spell authoritarian?' Jack Jr said at the back of Dad's head. 'A-D-O-R-N-O,' said Mum. Sometimes she's smart.

At Brunswick Heads we all cheered up again. The prawn trawlers were sliding down the estuary in a line, heading for the open sea. We stopped and watched them hump up and over the swells coming past the breakwater. There were seagulls and campers everywhere.

Population 8,000, said the sign back on the highway. 'And 80,000 in the hols,' said Dad.

Murwillumbah. Houses on stilts. 'There are those who think the Queensland border starts at Tweed Heads,' said Mum, 'and those who *know* it starts at Murwillumbah.'

'I can feel my neck turning red,' said Jack Jr.

The sun was going down when we reached Queensland. We couldn't see the border. The traffic was bumper to bumper all the way from Coolangatta through Kirra, Miami, Burleigh Heads, Palm Beach, Copocabana and Broadbeach.

When we finally got to Surfers all the skyscraper lights were on. It looked like Future City. The lights stretched all the way along the beachfront and shone on the sea. The reflections bounced about in the surf. I could hear trannie music tumbling along in the summer night air.

'It's falling into the ocean,' said Dad.

'Capitalism's last stand,' said Jack Jr.

'I like it,' I said.

'At least we're here,' said Mum.

Minnie yawned. 'Day trips are such a bore,' she said. 'Nothing ever happens.'

Commentaries (the day after):

Jack Jr: The trouble with this story is that it perpetuates the myth that it's possible to live a valid, resistant life as a sort of floating enclave within the capitalist system, whereas we know in fact that the system so dominates our lives it is impossible to escape it. Even the forms and styles of our attempts to escape are simply responses to the dominant order; I mean here's the family driving along in a hire-purchase car they don't even own, spending money they haven't yet earned, putting everything on credit, and ending up in the most vulgar symbol of contemporary capitalism of all – Surfers Paradise. Some escape! Like Douglas Stewart's *Silkworms*, they think they are free but they're not. The relationships in the family are all conventional: nuclear, male-dominated, hierarchical, a sort of reproduction at the personal level of the economic order – which is what you'd expect. The culture we swallow in the car and in the Big Banana is coercive and manipulative. My sisters seem to like everything indiscriminately – I've told 'em that before, but they're young. The argument doesn't do anything like justice to Adorno. I like my own parodic role in the story but the whole narrative is weighted against the reality of how things are.

Mum: I'm a bit sorry I'm reduced to Mum instead of being a real person. Art imitating life. Still, I liked the sense of community in the car, which in a way answers Jack Jr; we try to enact in our present lives what we demand of the future. That's the way we resist. Jack Jr's right about a lot of things but I think he's a bit pessimistic; if everything's as controlled as he says we might as well give up. Me, well, I think we've got to resist even if we think it's futile because it's the moral thing to do, and anyhow I don't really think it's futile, it's like kids' playdough, the social order reflects every thumbprint . . . also you can create alternatives . . . if it were impossible to resist in any way I can't see how you could ever have reform, revolution, any sort of change at all . . . the story *feels* like our family; it's pretty democratic despite Jack, Jack my husband . . . but he's learning, the kids have educated him . . . anyhow I've tried to explain to Jack Jr that of course we absorb everything around us but we modify it too, choose and reject . . . he's a bit determinist at the moment . . . testing it . . . I like the idea, though it's a bit fanciful, of a car full of cultural submachine guns . . . the story needs a sequel really . . . at the moment it's merely evocative because it presents a series of ironies.

Me: Well, I think the story's a bit unfair to me because I come across as a sort of gormless teenager who likes everything, except of course I do *see* everything even if I don't say much, which is how I sort of think I am, at the moment anyhow; also I like the way everyone's good-humoured, more or less, a long car trip can get you down; Dad's quite funny but I agree with Mum most of the time; Jack Jr's okay for a brother; I agree with a lot of what he says in the story because most of the stuff I see and listen to is junk, I know that; I just don't feel so fierce about it. I take what I like and leave the rest. Minnie's still working it out; I suppose I am too but I know one thing, it's going to change in my life because I'm going to change it. I think. The story describes the way things are for the moment, so it's got to be wrong.

Dad: I thought it was a story about a car trip.

Editor: I'm not sure the sequel works, but we'll leave it in for now.

Reader: (please fill in . . .)

Roadsigned 1992 by Richard Tipping.

wogs

ANIA WALWICZ   1982

'. . . wogs they don't look like you or me they look strange they are strange they don't belong here . . .'

The term 'wogs' has often been used by Australians of European origin to abuse any peoples who have more recently arrived from Europe or the Asian-Pacific region. This 'story' reproduces some of the voices of 'us' English-speaking Australians complaining about the peculiarities of 'them', the 'wogs'.

Ania Walwicz came to Australia from Poland when she was twelve. She is an artist as well as a writer.

Secondary school boys and girls, of various ethnic backgrounds, get along together in 'Teach Me to Dance', page 25.

they're not us they're them they're them they are else what you don't know what you don't know what they think they got their own ways they stick together you don't know what they're up to you never know with them you just don't know with them no we didn't ask them to come here they come and they come there is enough people here already now they crowd us wogs they give me winter colds they take my jobs they take us they use us they come here to make their money then they go away they take us they rip us off landlords they rise rent they take us they work too hard they take us they use us bosses we work in their factory rich wogs in wog cars rich jews in rich cars they take us they work so hard we are relaxed they get too much they own us they take my jobs away from me wogs they don't look like you or me they look strange they are strange they don't belong here they are different different skin colour hair they just don't look right they take us they land on us there isn't enough space for us now they come they work for less they can work in worse they take anything they work too hard they want from us we have to look after our own here not them let them go back where they come from to their own they're everywhere they get everywhere you can't speak to them why don't you learn to speak english properly they are not like you or me they're not the same as everybody they change us is your child educated by an australian? is it? do you know if? you don't know what they think you don't know what they can do here they change us they paint their houses blue green have you seen blue houses who ever heard of that they live too many together they're too noisy they chatter you don't know what they say they smell funny there's something funny about them strange not like you or me i don't want to see asian tram conductors they are not us not us they're them they're else what you don't know them nobody knows them they stick together they look after one another they don't care about us they're everywhere they're everywhere every day there's more of them we work in their factories they escape here we don't have to take them in this is our home they come we didn't ask them they spoil us they take us for what they can get they're not like us they behave different they're rude they act if they own the place they look wrong too dark too squat too short all wrong ugly too fat women go to fat dark skin monkeys i want to be with my own kind people like me exactly like me they stick out you can't miss them they're everywhere they shout they're noisy they're dirty they put vegetables in their front gardens they eat garlic they shouldn't have come here in the first place they're strangers i want to be with my own kind with my brothers with people like i am there's too many of them here already you don't know how to talk to them they're not clean they annoy me funny names luigi they got their own ways they don't do as you do they're aliens they look wrong they use us they take us they take us for what they can get from us then they go away they're greedy they take our space they not us not our kind they after what they can get they stick together i don't know what they say they don't fit in they dress wrong flashy they don't know our ways they breed and breed they take what little we got what is ours what belongs to us they take ours and ours they're not us

The Three-legged Bitch
ALAN MARSHALL   1968

'He had lived by killing. The death of dingoes brought him prestige, friendship, praise . . .'

A rugged old bushman, after a lifetime of trapping wild dogs, pursues one last sheep-killing dingo. What happens when the killers finally meet?

Despite being crippled by poliomyelitis as a child, Alan Marshall led an independent life travelling as a journalist and short story writer.

In 'Just Like That', page 81, a man also encounters and kills creatures of the wild.

Tim Sullivan was seventy-five years of age. He was a thickset, powerful man with a crown of grey hair. His face had weathered wind and sun and rain, and now bore the character of an old rock. He had calm blue eyes and spoke slowly, gathering words from a mind that had been given few opportunities to express itself in speech.

He lived in Jindabyne at the foothills of the Australian Alps. Everybody knew him. He had been a dogger, a dingo trapper, and the years of his youth and manhood had been spent with packhorses and dog traps among the mountains and high plains.

He had lived by killing. The death of dingoes brought him prestige, friendship, praise and sufficient money to live on. With the scalps of those he killed bagged on his packhorse, he would come down from the mountains to collect the bounties and replenish stores. He would ride down the main street of Jindabyne, his traps clinking from the back of the packhorse following him. Men standing at the hotel doorway would wave to him as he passed.

'How are ya, Tim?'

The station-owners, with their broad-brimmed hats and Harris tweed sports coats, shouted for him in pubs, threw him a fiver when some notorious dingo fell victim to his traps. They listened to his stories with interest, an interest born of an involvement with his successes and his failures. When on mustering rides they met him on lonely mountain tracks, they reined in their horses to yarn with him.

Imants Tillers, Australia, born 1950, *Mount Analogue*, 1985, oil stick, synthetic polymer paint on 165 canvas boards, 279.0 × 576.0 cm.

They vied with each other in offers of hospitality should he visit them to trap the dingoes that harassed their sheep.

'Spend a few weeks with me at Geehi, Tim.'

'There's always a room for you at Khancoban, Tim.'

He was a good fellow, an honest bloke, a chap you could rely on.

Upon the attitude of these men towards him, Tim Sullivan built a framework of confidence and pride in himself.

He had never known praise in his childhood. Now, as a man, his fame as a dogger brought him self-respect. It pleased him that educated and wealthy men spoke to him as an equal. It was his great achievement. It gave some meaning to his life, supported him in lonely moments when the howl of a dingo at night made him look up from his camp fire.

For fifty years he hunted dingoes. He followed them into remote valleys, along ridges few men had trod. He knew every cattle and sheep pad that bound the hills. He drove the few remaining dingoes back to the inaccessible places where they lived on wallabies and from where they were afraid to venture down to the sheep country. He acquired great skill and knowledge.

When Tim was sixty-five his wife died. She had been a placid, stout woman with a friendly manner. She wore aprons upon which she wiped her hands before offering one to your grasp. She would then bustle round the kitchen making tea, anxious to please his guest. The glance she sometimes gave her husband affirmed what he was saying.

He had always felt young when she was alive. He could lead his packhorse into the mountains and stay away a month tracking some elusive dingo. But he thought of his wife a lot. He was always happy to return, and felt a reluctance to leave again, to subject his stiffening joints to the sway of a saddle over miles of mountain tracks.

When she died he suddenly felt old. It was as if a cloak had been removed from him and he felt the coldness of the wind. His movements became slower, and from thinking ahead he began recalling the past.

'I can never sleep on Sunday nights. I keep thinking about when Nell was alive. Every Sunday we had a roast.'

He sold his horses and his traps. He became an old-age pensioner and hunted dingoes no longer. The attention of those people who noticed him walking up the street carrying a sugar-bag was momentarily arrested by his carriage.

'See that old bloke! He carries his head like he was somebody. I forget his name but he used to trap dingoes or something. They say he was famous at it. He keeps clean, doesn't he?'

He had been confident in the continuation of his friendships. But he was of no value to the station-owners now. He was finished out, done . . . He was an old-age pensioner who bored you with tales of your past losses. Gradually the men he had once served began to avoid him. They passed him on the street without a greeting. He began to realise where he now stood in the complex of the district's social structure.

'It sort of hurt me, him not recognising me. I spent a month at his place once. I was going to say to him, "Look, I'm not going to bite you for a couple of bob or the price of a drink. I just want to say 'hullo', that's all." But he just kept going.'

So it was – until the Three-legged Bitch came over from the Snakey Plains to harry the flocks in the Snowy River area.

For eight years the Three-legged Bitch roamed the ranges around the Snow Leases of the Kosciusko country. From the Grey Mare Range to the Pinch River men spoke of her. Her howl had been heard on the Big Boggy and they knew her tracks on the Thredbo. The bones of sheep she had slain lay along the banks of the Swampy Plains River on the Victorian side of the Snowy Mountains. She had crossed the Monaro Range, some sheepmen said.

The Three-legged Bitch was an outsize dingo with a thick rusty-red coat and a short bushy tail. When she was young and inexperienced she had been caught in a trap and one of her forepaws had been partly severed. Only one toe was left on this disfigured foot and the track it made was the brand by which she was known to those who hunted her.

She ran with a slight limp, her shoulder dropping a little when the leg she favoured took her weight. It had long since ceased to be the limp of pain or defective action; now it suggested a sinister development of style and her speed and strength seemed to stem from it.

She worked alone. Sometimes her howl brought a trotting male dog to a sudden halt on a valley track and he would stand a moment with lifted nose then turn and make up through the wooden spurs to the treeless uplands where she made her home.

But those wandering dogs who answered and went to her never possessed her cunning and they either fell victim to doggers or failed to survive long periods of hunger when the snow came.

On the crown lands above the timber where the tussocky grass grows thick and gentian flowers come in the Spring, sheepmen drive their flocks up from the valleys during the Summer months and leave them to graze on areas they have leased from the government – Snow Leases, they are marked on the maps that define them.

When the first horsemen appeared on the high plains the Three-legged Bitch would retire into the remote parts where they could not follow her. From here she came out to kill.

In March, before Winter begins, the sheepmen go in and bring their flocks down to the snow-free valleys round the homesteads where the wild dogs never go.

There are no sheep on top in the Winter and then the snow lies in heavy drifts on the Snowy Plains and the dingoes and wild dogs grow lean with hunger. Yet the Three-legged Bitch always retained her strength. Some said she raided the rubbish dumps of the tourist chalets on those wild nights when her tracks would be covered by morning. A few doggers – those who delayed leaving the high valleys until snow forced them out – suspected she lived on sheep missed in the annual muster. These animals are often buried in the snow and here the Three-legged Bitch would scent them as she trotted through the still, white world of the surface. When the warm breath of them came to her through the snow she burrowed down until she reached them huddled together in terror. Then she tore the living flesh from their backs.

In the Summer she came in about every third night, favouring boisterous nights when terrified bleating would be lost in the wind and her panting was just another sound. She had been known to slaughter fifty sheep in one run when there was a gale and a full moon was whipped by clouds. She had killed for a week at Thompson's when Thompson was away.

All the sheepmen knew her work. She always revealed her identity in the method of her killing. She was the criminal betrayed by 'fingerprints'. Long before she became known as 'The Three-legged Bitch' tales were told of sheep with mangled throats lying in lines on the snow leases of the high country. The unknown dog that slew them ran on the offside of each panic-stricken victim until, in that stumbling moment of weakness for which it awaited, it leapt for the throat, jerking the head backward as its teeth sank deep, and breaking the animal's neck as it came down.

Sheep still alive but gasping horribly through torn windpipes were brought in at the muster. Many sheep were never found. Their torn bodies lay in ravines and among rocks where their last frantic run had taken them.

Angry men held quick musters and swore at the count. In the bars of mountain pubs, with the froth of beer on their stubbly lips, they slew the Three-legged Bitch with fury.

'I'll fix her once I get hold of her.'

'If she gets amongst my ewes I'll follow her to the Murray.'

She robbed them of money and for this they hated her. Each murderous raid she made, each new killing, created in the minds of those whose sheep had died from her teeth a picture of a new and more ferocious dog, an animal governed by human passions of revenge and hate, one that for some strange personal reason had selected them as victims of her vendetta.

The kill of minor dingoes was blamed on her; kills twenty miles apart did not save her from a double accusation.

'She killed at Groggin's Gap on Wednesday.'

'She came in to Big Boggy on Wednesday.'

All slaughtered sheep were hers; the kill of every dog was hers.

She killed for sport, they said. She was blood-hungry, blood-mad . . . She snarled and drove in, she ripped down then back, she leaped like a shadow, whipped round and in again, on to another one. Snarl and rip and slash and on again. This was how they saw her, flecked with blood, her snarling mouth dripping. This was how they described her one to another, from man to man, across bar counters, in sheds and homes. The instinct that drove her to kill as many sheep as she could in a run seemed to them evidence of a creature with the mind of a murderer.

Before sheep had come to this country kangaroos and wallabies had been the dingoes' food. These animals could outrun the hunting dogs. It was only when an unsuspecting mob of wallabies was quietly feeding near trees or sheltering rocks that they were in danger. The hiding dingo suddenly burst into view fully extended and was among them with ripping teeth before they had time to gather speed. Two or three would die before the mob bounded away.

Food was life. Survival demanded the seizing of every opportunity to kill, for such opportunities did not come every day. Two slain wallabies were food for days.

Then sheep came to the mountains, helpless animals that could not escape by running. So the dingoes killed until they were tired, driven to slaughter one after another, not by a mind finding a savage joy in killing but by an instinct born thousands of years before when the animals they hunted had the speed to escape them.

The Three-legged Bitch had survived because of her skill in obtaining food, by her skill in avoiding the guns and traps and poisons of man.

She was afraid of men but there lingered in her some allegiance to them handed down from remote times when her domesticated ancestors had reached Australia with the first dark man. Sometimes from a safe distance she followed the cattle-drovers or a solitary musterer. She stood far back from the light of campfires, howling quaveringly as she watched them.

She was the last of her kind in those parts, the only pure-bred dingo that had survived the hunting of men. Yet she was incapable of feelings of revenge. That feeling marked the attitude of men towards her, the men from whose vast flocks she had taken food.

For eight years the trappers hunted her. First for the price of her hide, then for the value of her scalp, then for twenty pounds reward . . . fifty . . . a hundred . . . They came up from the farms and the towns and the cities. There were young men with brown faces and strong arms and old men with beards. They came leading packhorses or tramping up through the woolly-butt and snow-gums carrying guns. Solitary riders with the stock of a cocked gun resting on their thigh walked their horses through the timber, across plains of snow-grass, down long ravines, their heads turning from side to side in an eager seeking. Packs of dogs, noses to the ground, followed in the confident steps of owners seeking a final payment. From some of the laden horses stumbling along the high tracks huge dog-traps clanked and swung. Men came with poison, with pellets of dough and ground glass, with stakes and snares. They shot brumbies and with bloodstained gloves upon their hands thrust poisonous crystals into the gashes made in the flanks. They poisoned the carcasses of sheep, cattle . . . Groups of sheepmen rode in lines, shouting through the scrub. On the far side their companions waited with guns.

She watched them come and go.

The defeated men came down from the mountains with tales that made minor triumphs of their failures. They lied to save their pride, they boasted to impress.

'I bowled her over with my second shot,' Ted Arthur said. 'She was staggering when she got up. I reckon she'd toss it in somewhere round by Little Twynam.'

He didn't say how he came upon her at a kill on the Grey Mare Range, how he fired and missed. She went down that slope in long bounds, hugging the cover, with his kangaroo-dog at her heels, then shot into a clump of wattle. When Ted's spurred horse reached the clump the Three-legged Bitch glided out on the far side and disappeared into the scrub. It was then he found his dog thrashing in a circle on the bloody leaves.

She had thrown up three of Bluey Taylor's baits, and Jack Bailey always swore she lost another toe in one of his traps.

But they all came down – Ted and Bluey and Jack and scores of others. They all left the snow leases, left the mountains.

Five men visited Tim one day. They left their cars at the gate and stood in a group before his door, waiting for it to be opened to their knock. Tim invited them in. He knew them all. Once he had imagined they were his friends. They still were, it seemed, by the warmth of their handshakes and the tone of their voices.

'We want to talk to you about the Three-legged Bitch, Tim,' said one. 'She killed seven of my ewes last night and Jack here lost five on Friday night. We've got to do something about it fast. She scatters those she doesn't kill and God only knows how many we have lost. You are the only man who can get her, Tim. We want you to go after her. It won't take you so long with your experience. Now wait till you hear our proposition,' he hastened to add as Tim moved to speak. 'We know you have retired from the game, so to speak, but . . .'

They all paid tribute to his skill as a dogger. Everybody said he was the only man who would bring in her scalp. They were all agreed on this. They would stake him, buy his grub, supply him with horses and packs, pay him a hundred pounds for her scalp. He was still remarkably fit. You only had to look at him. They recalled him coming down from the top in snow storms, they remembered the time he had ridden ninety-four miles between sunrise and sunset.

'You couldn't kill him with an axe,' one remarked to another.

They continued to praise him, but Tim wasn't listening. He was looking at the walls of his hut. Many things hung there, all with a tongue – an old bridle, a rusty broken trap, the skin of a dingo, faded photographs in frames of painted cork, frames of seashells, pictures of horses cut from the pages of magazines . . . How many times had he sat and looked at them! It was his life he looked at and it was a protection. He only had to turn his head and there through the window were the mountains with a thin track winding up into the cold and the loneliness, the loneliness that had often sat with him in this room.

'You couldn't kill him with an axe,' he thought.

Their words were sweet to him. The pains, the aches, the digestive troubles his mind had fashioned from boredom and which seemed to lurk within him awaiting the trigger of purposelessness to release them, suddenly vanished and a deep breath filled his lungs with a new strength. He'd show them, these men who could discard a friendship like an old shirt. They needed him now. All the others had failed. He wouldn't fail.

'I'll bring you back her hide,' he said.

They took him down to the pub and shouted for him. They gave him advice. They all knew how the bitch could be caught.

'You'd probably bring her into the traps using piss as a lure,' said one of the men, a grazier whose wife, tired of life in the bush, was living in a Melbourne flat. 'They'll follow the trail for miles.'

Tim didn't reply. He knew all the lures. Tie a bitch on heat so that she has to stand on a sheet of galvanised iron, catch her urine in a tin and bottle it – it would lure a male dingo into the traps or within reach of a rifle, but didn't this bloke realise he was dealing with a slut? It had no appeal to her.

His mind even now was planning the methods he would use. He was remembering past triumphs when with unresented patience he followed a dog for months until he knew its every habit, its peculiarities, its weaknesses . . . He would do the same again.

Four days later he was following Barlees Track across Reads Flat. The Geehi flowed nearby, fed by the melting snow that still lay in drifts on the Snowy Mountains. He was making for a cattleman's hut not far from Wild Cow Flats where the tracks of the Three-legged Bitch had been seen by several sheepmen preparing to take their flocks up above the tree-line to graze during the Summer months.

She had not yet killed, they said, though one of the men who had seen her several times trotting down from the Grey Mare Range said she was in good condition after the Winter.

'She knows when you haven't got a gun,' he said. 'She stood and watched me one day – only about forty yards away. You could tell what she was thinking.'

For two months Tim camped in the hut. He used it as a base from where he ranged the surrounding country. He had found her tracks, listened to her howl as he sat over his log fire.

He thought a lot about her while sitting before his fire. He developed a strange affection for her. *Was* she as merciless and cruel as they said? *Was* she evil? He had earned his living by killing. And he had got joy from it. He had looked down on the trapped dog with excitement. Then he had killed. Now he didn't like thinking about this. He didn't like thinking how he loved the admiration of other men, an admiration earned by killing.

'There's nothing you don't know about dingoes.'

'I'll hand it to you – you're the best dogger in Australia.'

Then he had seen her. He had been riding back with a load of stores he had bought at Jindabyne when he came to an outcrop of rock just off the track. Huge boulders leaning one against the other formed cavities that made a perfect shelter. He dismounted, left his reins hanging and began searching around the rocks for tracks. The indentation of each claw was always absent from her tracks. They had been worn down by age and travel and she left only the impression of her pads. The claw tracks of young dogs were always deeply impressed into the ground.

She had been there all right. He looked at her tracks. She was older than he thought. He noticed the mark of her injured paw. He turned and looked up the mountain side as if expecting to see her slinking among the boulders. Suddenly she shot from a cavity to the left of him. She bounded on to a flat rock and then stood looking at him for a few swift heartbeats. His gun was back with the horses. Then she was gone. She seemed to flow over the rock upon which she had been standing. She glided through the trees and rocks making of each one a cover that stood between them.

Tim saw her many times over the next few months. He got to know her well. She had a deep curiosity. She often studied him from the shelter of some rock on the mountain side before slipping quietly away. He had seen other dogs, too, mongrels with her blood in them. But he was not involved with them. He had set out to destroy one animal – the dingo bitch. She was famous, so was he.

He studied her for months. He knew she always came in fairly fast. She trotted along a track, her head low, her tongue dripping. She never paused but kept up her tireless trot for miles. She always went out by a different track.

When making back to the higher country she went slowly, pausing to roll on the grass or sniff at a tree-trunk she knew would attract other dingoes. She walked and her hunger was satisfied.

When coming in on wild moonlight nights, she sometimes stopped and raised her head and her throat would vibrate in a quavering howl, a sound that always gave Tim a disturbing feeling of fear. His reaction to the howl of a dingo had never been removed by familiarity with the sound. The uncomforted voice of the bitch drew him into an experience of utter loneliness. It was the cry of a living thing in isolation and it united his yearnings with her own.

He discovered an old sheep track coming down from the craggy top of the range where it ended on a treeless flat. Here sheep were often grazing. He set two traps on this track. He set them with skill and left them. Some day she would use that track. Months of rain and sun would remove all evidence of their existence. They would wait.

He sought the sheep tracks she had used recently. On one that followed the crest of a spur he found her tracks, clear and distinct, unweathered by rain and wind. She always trotted along ridges rather than through valleys. She liked open country for travel and avoided those tracks that demanded she cross a creek. She was always reluctant to leave a cattle or sheep pad on which she found herself. She followed them for miles lifting her front legs high in a style that had been cultivated on the tussocky uplands above the tree-line. On this track Tim set his traps in the form of a letter 'H'. He selected a spot where the track was flanked by bleached tussocks that formed a dense cover she would naturally avoid.

The dog-traps Tim was carrying were like oversized rabbit-traps, each with two springs. The teeth of the wide jaws did not meet. This prevented the dog's leg from being severed instead of held.

Tim wore old gloves which were caked with the dried blood of a brumby. He spread a bag on the track, placed a trap beside it, then cut an outline round the trap with an old shearblade, pushing the blade deep into the soil. He removed the outlined sod by prising it free with the blade until it could be lifted intact and placed carefully on the bag. He placed the topsoil on one corner, the bottom soil on another so that he could return them to their original position in the set. The set trap fitted exactly into the excavation.

He enjoyed doing this. All his past experiences were directing him and they grew in value as he pondered on his skill and knowledge. He suddenly felt linked with all men who knew their craft and worked well, a great army of men with whom he walked shoulder to shoulder.

He never touched the soil. He transferred each root-bound lump with the blade. Beneath the raised plate he thrust dry grass, pushing it carefully into position to prevent soil collecting there. He did not place paper above the plate as in rabbit trapping. It would be likely to rustle when a dog stepped close to it.

He buried the chains attached to the traps with the same care. At the end of each chain a strand of wire increased its length and ended by being fastened to a 'drag', a log of wood Tim had selected because of its shape. They were not too heavy and would enable the dingo to drag them some distance without subjecting her leg to a strain that would sever it.

When the traps and chains were covered he carried the bag on which surplus soil was lying and shook it some distance away. He then used the bag to 'blow' the set. He waved the bag above the set blowing away loose crumbs of earth. Using the shearblade he scattered dry leaves and broken cow manure above the area on which he had been working until all evidence of his work had vanished.

He stood up and looked down at his work with satisfaction. The longer the traps stayed in the ground the better his chance of catching her.

He passed near the set two days later but it hadn't been disturbed, then on the fourth day after a gusty night of wind he reined his horse beside the track and looked down on the scarified earth over which he had worked so carefully. Two of the traps were sprung. Dirt and stones had been scratched over them in what seemed to be a gesture of contempt. She had come trotting down the track, following it with her head down. She had continued between the arms of the 'H' then stopped dead at the bar. Here she had stood a moment deadly still – the last four pawmarks were deeply indented – sniffing at the polluted air. She had then backed carefully out, stepping into the tracks she had already made, until she was free of the enclosure. It was here she had turned and ripped up the stones and earth in an attempt to render the hidden steel harmless. Tim sat on his horse and looked at her answer. There was a faint smile on his face.

In the months that followed he tried every trick he knew. Wearing gloves stained with blood he had dropped poisonous crystals into slashes made in the flanks of freshly-killed brumbies. He had shot only thin horses. He believed a dingo, knowing it had swallowed poison, could throw up the flesh of a fat horse. She had eaten round the slashes. He tried poisoning the carcasses of sheep she had slain. She ignored them.

But still she killed, leaving a trail of dead animals on the Swampy Plain, out by Bogong, on the slopes of the Blue Cow. She was killing with more than usual ferocity as if danger had made her desperate.

He dragged putrid legs of sheep by a rope tied to his saddle, leading her for miles to baits of fresh liver with deadly mouths slashed into them. She often followed these trails, scratching dirt over each bait as she reached it. On one occasion she had carried two of the baits and dropped them on top of a third that lay on an open pad beneath the sun. Beside this pile of poisoned meat she had left her dung.

A further symbol of her contempt? Tim kicked it to one side and smiled. She had no mind for such gestures. It was the heavy odour of putrid flesh that inspired her to leave the smell of her presence for the benefit of other dogs.

On a small flat open to the sky Tim found a pool of clear water. The banks were undermined, and matted dry grass clung to these banks and hung over the water immersing their pale, brittle stems beneath the surface. On one side there was a gap in the encircling grass and here on a tiny beach of grey mud she had left the imprint of her battered paws.

Tim studied them, then looked around him. The flat was treeless except for a bushy snow gum growing some twenty yards away. He knew that after a dingo drank she would trot to the nearest tree where she would stand or lie down for a while in the shade. There were no tracks to the tree – the grass was too thick – but there was an impress on the grass beneath it that suggested she had lain there.

He set four traps around the tree. When he had finished, the grass, the earth, the littered bark were as if no hand had touched them. He was pleased and stood for a moment anticipating victory.

Two days later he stood there again. She had sprung the tracks with scratched dirt. She had drunk at the spring, trotted to the tree and stood there a moment with senses alert while her sensitive nose detected the evidence of his work. Then the fear and the destruction of what she feared. Tim understood her. He loaded the traps on to his horse and rode away and there was no anger nor resentment in him.

He followed her with a rifle and fired at her from distances that demanded keener eyes than he possessed to hit her. He watched the spurt of dust rise near her feet then trailed her until her tracks petered out among the rocks that littered the uplands.

She became increasingly wary of him – she feared guns and rifles – and he began finding it difficult to get within sight of her. He moved from hut to hut on the high country, following reports of her killing, and camping for weeks in some remote shelter built by cattlemen and only visited for a week or two each year.

He wintered at the Geehi Hut on the track to Khancoban. He packed in his stores and was never short of tucker. He was used to solitude. When Spring came to the mountains he followed the retreating snow to the top. For a week he searched for her tracks then found them criss-crossing the pitted earth behind a flock of climbing sheep. She had killed one of the stragglers.

There were moments when he felt she was indestructible, that all his skill was useless against her instinct to survive. He sometimes felt there wasn't a trail from the top in which he hadn't buried his traps; no clearing he hadn't baited.

He had made it a habit to make a regular visit to the old trail in which he had set his traps when first he came to the mountains. Almost a year had passed since he had hidden them beneath the track she once had made. Snow had covered them since then; bleak winds had flattened the soil above them, sun and rain and frost had removed all trace of man and the track wound upwards in an unbroken line that smelt of wild grass and the presence of Spring.

His mare knew the way. She moved at a brisk walk through the tussocks while he sat relaxed in the saddle, the reins drooping from her neck. He had no feeling of anticipation. This visit had become a habit.

When he first saw her crouched upon the track, draggled, panting, surrounded by the torn earth of her struggling, he experienced a leap of excitement that was almost a pain, so intense it was. The air had no motion and he sat in a still silence savouring his triumph. He could hear distant shouts of acclaim from beyond the accusing mountains, cheering . . .

The moment passed and his shoulders sagged to the burden of the accusation. He alighted from the mare and walked to her. Two traps held her helpless, their naked jaws clamped on a front and hind leg. They had lain in darkness beneath the track for more than a year and the smell of the earth had become their smell. The chains were taut from the drags which had prevented her from struggling into the concealing grass.

As he approached she wriggled backwards taking up what slack was available to her, then she faced him, crouching low, her muzzle resting on the earth, her fangs bared in a soundless snarl.

They confronted each other, the old man and the greying dingo, both killers who had reached a final reckoning. And Tim knew it in a clouded way. Hundreds of slain dingoes marked the trail of his lonely passage. Her pathway was a line of torn sheep lying motionless across the mountain uplands where she was born. He was surprised that she didn't reveal in her appearance the murderer of her reputation. Sheepmen saw her as inspired by an evil joy in slaughter. The mind that directed her was to them the cold and calculating instrument of a criminal. Now Tim saw her as a lonely old dingo scarred by pellets of shot, by traps and the teeth of hunters' dogs. He was a bit like that himself, he thought, but his scars didn't show. They lay beneath the confident smile, the pride in killing; hers denied him his pride.

'I'll bring you back her hide,' he had told them.

But when I kill her, he reflected, I kill myself. I'll go back to being an old-age pensioner. No more slaps on the back, shouting in pubs. No more invitations to stay at the homesteads of wealthy graziers. I'll return to my hut and die in my hut and that will be the end of it all.

He stood watching her, torn by indecision. He wanted to go on living with himself, he wanted to be able to walk with his head up, with dignity. When he did act it was with sudden desperation. Reason had bowed its head.

He seized a heavy stick and advanced upon her, his face twisted with an anguish his powerful arms denied. She waited for him, shrinking closer to the earth, her glaring eyes desperate. The snarl she had held in silence now found voice in a vibrating growl of defiance and she sprang as he raised the stick aloft. She took up the slack of both chains in her spring and the blow he brought to the side of her head jerked her sideways as the tightened chains arrested her leap. She fell on her side to the ground, her head thrown back, her four legs taut and quivering.

He hit her again, not with frenzy but with a kind of despair, then turned and walked back to his mare. He suddenly felt old and tired and he walked stiffly. With his head resting against the saddle he drew deep breaths of replenishment until the cold sense of betrayal passed and he could stand erect.

He walked back to her body lying prone on the ground and released her paws from the grip of the traps. He dragged her to one side, her head bouncing loosely over the stones. Her worn teeth were bared in one last horrible grimace from which Tim turned his eyes.

He'd made up his mind. He buried her there beneath the tussocky grass and he did it with the same care he used in setting a trap. When he straightened up, the grass was waving in the mountain wind above her grave and the sheep track was the same as it was before he'd strewn it with death. Cloud shadows rippled up the mountain side like the quick and silent passing of her feet, and an eagle soared down the wind.

It was a good place to rest.

Miriam Stannage, Australia, born 1939, *Morse Code Series (SOS* · · · − · · ·*)*, *Salt Lake*, 1990, cibachrome photograph, 76 × 52 cm.
Collection: National Gallery of Australia, Canberra.

We Like White-man Alright

BILL NEIDJIE   1989

Bill Neidjie was born in the Kakadu area of northern Australia where
he still lives. In this talk with Keith Taylor, who recorded Bill Neidjie's
exact words, he tells something of Australia's history as it looks to an
Aboriginal man. And he shares what he fears and hopes and values for
his people, their land and their culture now. Readers who are used to
short stories written by white Westerners may need to listen carefully
to this tale which has a very different, looser form, more like a
conversation.

Like Bill Neidjie, a number of Aboriginal storytellers live in
communities which continue to share their stories and culture in
spoken, not written words. Now many of these stories are being
written down for others outside the teller's own society. However,
something of the sounds, the rhythms, the flow, of conversation still
comes through in this story, especially when it is read aloud.

The language may seem strange to many who are not familiar with
this kind of English. It may help to remember that it is not an incorrect
version of standard English but a variety in its own right, with its own
vocabulary and grammar. Aboriginal Englishes are used by their
speakers to communicate their culture and their experiences of living
in a country colonised by whites.

Where they say we rich.
Yes, we rich alright . . . not really!
Aborigine e rich man e got change clothes, clean clothes,
look pretty-boy, yes.
But me I think . . .
Aborigine had chain in the neck first go!

First Aborigine e saw it white-Man . . .
e put it people, chain longa neck
because they pinch it cattle.
They shouldn't.
They get police . . . e put chain.
Now . . . court they take im in but before . . . chain.

Wild, wild people.
They never see white-man.
They said . . .
   'They might run away.
   We can't catch im. Too many bushes.'

So they put chain.

But wasn't Aborigine fault.
White-European didn't make friend with Aborigine.
That first go e put chain!

But what about White-European they coming in this world?
What about that chain in the leg?
They row . . . long chain everyone of them.
Same thing. They was prisoner too!
Before they came this everyone bin have im chain.
Now all bin settle now . . . settle down.

Should be missionaries first they started
and asking people this culture.
What they done?
They run it quick!

They brought in something too . . . drinking.
Before, they should first ask question
about dreaming, story, cave, people.
They bin rush in.
They took up school . . . teach.
Now Aborigine losing it now.
They lose it already, I know,
I guess that.
And they running drinking.
They should be keep for a while . . . after.
No . . . they was too quick.
So wasn't Aborigine fault . . . White-European fault.

That missionary e telling Bible there . . .
   'Oh you got to remember up there
   and you got to be become good.'

Same thing Aborigine if lot of story.
I used to go church but I hang on this.
Because I can't say liar . . . e's true.
E's very true this story.

We know White-European got different story.
But our story, everything dream,
dreaming, secret, 'business' . . .
you can't lose im.
This story you got to hang on for you,
children, new children, no-matter new generation
and how much new generation.
You got to hang on this old story because the earth,
this ground, earth where you brought up,
this earth e grow, you growing little by little,
tree growing with you too, grass . . .

I speaking story
and this story you got to hang on, no matter who you,
no-matter what country you.
You got to understand . . . this world for us.
We came for this world.

We say we don't like each other.
Ahh . . . no good we don't like each other. What for?
E not from somewhere else!

That why you stand for it.
No-matter who different, different country . . .
all same thing.

We like white-man alright. We like im city
but city make you sick of it. Better this . . .
no-matter little house, little road
and others where no road,
e can see something there, green, tree . . .

Now e's lovely over there.
E's feeling now . . . wind . . . e coming.
Now we telling story e start blow.

E pumping now that leaf, that blood there.
E not wood but you'n'me that.
E man but e listen for you'n'me. E listen.

Yesterday I feel it because I was tired
and last night . . . oh, I feel it terrible, I nearly dead.
Because I never come put im this story.
I feel it yesterday afternoon too . . . no wind . . . no story!
Today e feeling now.
That wind e love, love, love.
I love wind.
E blowing . . . nice country in the plain.

E can blow.
Star . . . e can look.
All the same, all same.
You can't change it.
That world e was like that now.

This Law, country, people . . .
no-matter who you people,
red, yellow, black and white . . .
but the blood is same.
Country, you in other place
But exactly blood, bone . . . e same.

And all my people all dead
but we got few, that's all.
Not much, not many . . . getting too old
and young-fellas I don't know they hang on this story.

All my uncle gone
but this story I got im.
They told me, taught me
and I can feeling.
Feeling with my blood or body,
feeling all this tree and country.
While you sitting down e blow,
you feel it wind

and same this country you can look
but feeling make you.

Feeling make you out there with wind, open place
because e coming through your body
because you're like that.
Have a look while e blow, tree
and you feeling with your body
because tree just about like your brother or father
and tree watching you.

Someone can't tell you.
Story e telling you yourself.
E tell you how you feel because tree or earth
because you brought up with this earth,
tree, eating, water.

That way they give us talk.

So I'm saying now,
earth is my mother or my father.
I'll come to earth.
I got to go same earth
and I'm sitting on this dirt is mine
and children they playing.
Tree is mine.
In my body that tree.

This story I'm telling it
because I was keeping secret myself.
I was keeping in my mind with the culture
and see other people what they was doing
and I was feeling sad you know.
White-European different story
what we new generation now,
different story.
Because school doing it and something else
and our people they forget that.
They going little by little.

They shouldn't be, they not supposed to,
should be the man with the pressure . . .
put it on this.
No-matter about that White-European,
e can go with that one
but must White-European got to be listen this culture
and this story
because important one this.

Detail from *The National Picture*, 1985, by Geoff Parr, Nekko print on canvas.

Glossary

angophora	tree, also called the coastal red gum. It has twisted branches and in windy places it can become stunted and nearly as wide as it is tall.
baklava	Greek pastry layered with nuts and covered with honey syrup.
banksia	bush with leathery leaves and dense flower spikes like a bottle brush. The plant takes its name from Joseph Banks, the English botanist who accompanied Captain Cook on his voyages of exploration in the Pacific region in the late eighteenth century.
blackboy	grass tree with a dark stem and a head of long grassy leaves.
boomer	male kangaroo.
boong	highly insulting name for an Aboriginal person. It was also used to refer to the indigenous people of New Guinea and Malaysia when Australian troops were in that area of the Pacific during the Second World War. The word may come from an Aboriginal word, or from an Indonesian word for 'elder brother'.
boya	word for money in the Aboriginal language, Nyungar, spoken in the south-west of Western Australia.
break, fire break	a wide strip of land in areas of dense bush cleared of trees and undergrowth to halt or break the advance of a bushfire.
brumby	one of the many wild horses that roam free in the open outback areas of Australia. Where the word originated is not known for certain, though it may come from a Captain or Major Brumby, who had a reputation in the early nineteenth century as a horse breaker.
camp	land set aside as an Aboriginal settlement.
cocky	person who owns a small farm. The word comes from 'cockatoo', a large, noisy parrot with a crest of feathers.
corroboree	traditional Aboriginal gathering, often accompanied by music and dancing.
cut out	the 'cut out' is the end of the annual sheep-shearing on a

	farm, when the work for shearers 'cuts out' or finishes.
dag	person who is socially awkward, who lacks style; such a person's looks or manner are called 'daggy'.
deli	abbreviated form of 'delicatessen'. A deli is a small neighbourhood shop which sells a wide range of groceries and is open from early morning until late evening.
dingo	wolf-like native dog, domesticated by Aboriginal people, which roams country areas.
dings	word used by surfers for dents in their boards.
Dreaming, the	sometimes called 'the Dreamtime'. In Aboriginal belief, this refers to the time of spirit beings which created or became the features of the natural world. The stories told of those beings are not myths of long ago, because the Aboriginal people have not thought about history as Europeans do; to them the past does not go before the present but rather is contained within it. The Dreaming sets up a spiritual relationship between people and the land with its plants and animals and is the basis of the traditional Aboriginal way of life.
droog	term from the novel *A Clockwork Orange* but is used more generally to refer to groups of adolescents who hang about on the streets and dress and act in ways that set them apart from mainstream culture.
dunny	shed containing an outdoor lavatory, found in unsewered areas. It was often some distance from the house. Nowadays such a building may be laughed at as belonging to an earlier, less sophisticated era. For example, something or someone isolated may be called 'as lonely as a country dunny'.
Everage, Edna	character invented by the stage comedian Barry Humphries, Edna was originally an 'average' suburban housewife, cheerfully vulgar, overbearing and talkative. More recently she has gone up in the world to become Dame Edna.
foamies	surf boards made of plastic foam.
gelati	Italian water-based ice confection now popular among Australians of many cultural backgrounds.
Ghan	name of the train between Adelaide and Alice Springs. 'Ghan' refers to the Afghan camel drivers who maintained

supplies in those remote outback areas in the days before road, rail and air transport became prevalent.

gidgee scrub	gidgee is a variety of bushy wattle trees.
goanna	large lizard.
grappa	alcohol, like brandy, made from grapes.
guernsey	football jersey, usually sleeveless, worn by Australian Rules football players. (Australian Rules is a football game played by eighteen a side with an oval ball.) Originally the British word came from Britain and referred to a knitted, close-fitting garment worn by seamen. These days in Australia, 'get a guernsey' can mean to become a member of any kind of group, or to be marked out for some honour.
hovea	shrub with blue pea-like flowers.
humpy	Aboriginal word for a temporary shelter, made by covering a simple frame of branches with bark, grass or leaves. Now it often refers to any makeshift dwelling, especially one made of rough or salvaged materials.
kalimera	'Good day' in Greek.
Kingswood	large sedan model of the Holden, an Australian-made car.
koordah	'brother' or 'friend' in the Western Australian Aboriginal language.
lamington	cube of sponge cake dipped in chocolate icing and rolled in shredded coconut, named in honour of Lord Lamington, who was the Governor of Queensland in the late nineteenth century. These days it is often laughed at as typically Australian and unsophisticated or bourgeois.
lantana	tough, flowering, twiggy shrub.
larrikin	word imported from England in the nineteenth century, where it meant a mischievous young man or a hooligan. In Australia it could refer to a member of a town street gang or to a rowdy young man in the country. Nowadays it can also mean someone who is willing to ignore social conventions and 'proper' behaviour.
Menzies	Robert Menzies was the Prime Minister of Australia and leader of the conservative Liberal Party between 1944 and 1966. Many people now see those years as a period when Australians were very narrow-minded and very English in

their ways. (Menzies was very keen to strengthen his country's ties with Britain).

metal	broken stone or shingle surface of a road.
metho	methylated spirits, drunk as a cheap substitute for other forms of alcohol.
M.T.T.	Adelaide public transport bus depot.
North Shore	respectable, wealthy suburbs on the northern side of Sydney Harbour.
Nyoongah	word which Aboriginal people of the south-west of Western Australia use to refer to themselves. (Aboriginal people in other areas have different words to refer to themselves).
prickly moses	prickly shrub that belongs to the wattle family (acacia).
re-entry	surfing manoeuvre in which the surfer heads up into, and comes over with, a wave as it breaks.
roll	roll of bank notes.
scrub	rough undergrowth of native plants in the bush, or the area covered with such growth. When European settlers used this term, like 'bush', they were not distinguishing the large variety of plants it was made up of, and so it was easier for them to regard it as worthless and fit for getting rid of.
shed	shearing shed; the term is also used of the period during which shearing takes place there.
sickie, take a	day's sick leave from a paid job. This refers particularly to someone taking a day off without being really sick. Many shortened words in Australian slang have this kind of ending, such as 'mozzie' for mosquito, or 'tinnie' for a can of beer.
spencer	long-sleeved close-fitting vest knitted from cotton or wool, worn under outer clothing.
spinifex	spiky tussock grass, often found in dry regions.
stubby	short, squat beer bottle, usually holding 375ml.
Trots, the	races in which horses trot pulling a driver in a light two-wheeled vehicle. Spectators often bet on the winners.
unna	Aboriginal word that often comes at the end of a question, meaning something like 'Isn't it?' or 'Is that so?'.
wadgula	white people in the Aboriginal language of south-western Australia.

wallaby	any of the smaller kinds of animals in the kangaroo family. The word was taken from an Aboriginal language in the Sydney area and was one of the first to find its way into English.
wank, wanking	self-indulgent or egotistical behaviour.
wattle	shrubs or trees belonging to the acacia family. A very great variety of wattles grows in all areas of the country. Their fluffy yellow balls of pollen-laden stamens are one of Australia's national emblems.
Whitlam, Gough	Prime Minister of Australia 1972–75 and leader of the socialist Labour Party between 1967 and 1978. It was a boom time of building, when people had great confidence in Australia's prosperity in the present and future.
woodarchi	evil spirit. Aboriginal people thought of woodarchis as small hairy men with red eyes or else with feather-feet.
woolly-butt	group of eucalypt trees which have thick fibrous bark on the lower part of their trunks.
woolshed rouseabout	labourer who helps shearers by cleaning up clippings, etc.